DISCOVERED IN THE DARK

Discovered in the Dark

J.J. KANG

DISCOVERED IN THE DARK by J.J. Kang
Copyright © 2025 by J.J. Kang
All rights reserved.

The story, all names, characters, and incidents portrayed in this production are fictitious. No identification with actual persons (living or deceased), places, buildings, and products is intended or should be inferred.

ISBN-13 Paperback: 979-8-9904829-3-7
ISBN-13 Hardback: 979-8-9904829-4-4
ISBN-13 E-Book: 979-8-9904829-5-1

Book Cover by Asterielly Designs [www.asteriellydesigns.com]
Interior Formatting by Mariska Maas — Rubre Art [www.rubreart.com]
Developmental and Line Edits by Earley Editing [www.earleyediting.com]

1000 CRANES PRESS
www.jayjaykang.com

First Edition 2025

To the people in our lives we'd go to the ends of the world for.

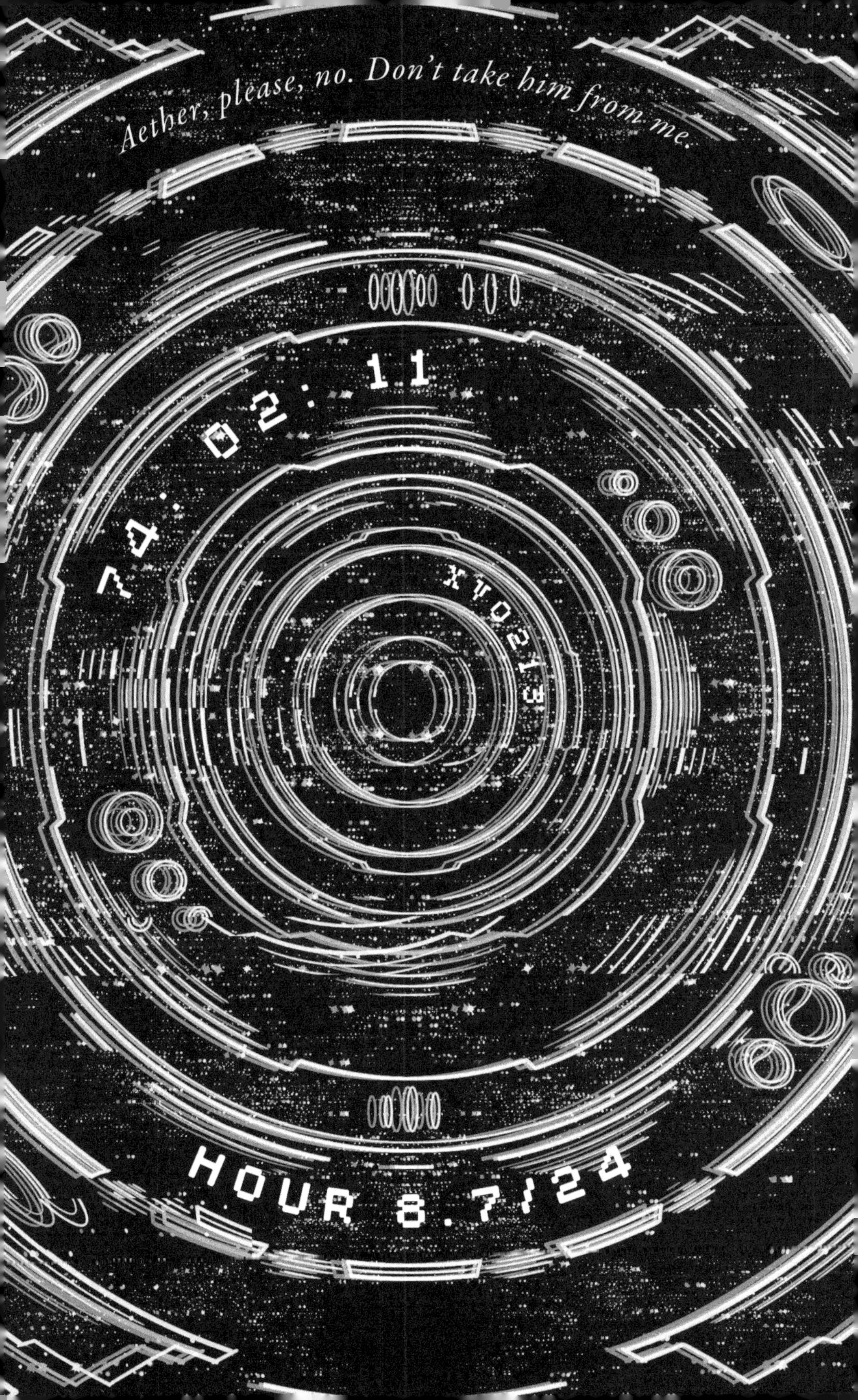

Aether, please, no. Don't take him from me.
24. 02: 11
XV0213
HOUR 8.7/24

- ONE -

Death was like falling asleep.

That's what Kennex was told, at least. Experiencing it himself, he disagreed. The pain alone was enough to make the comparison laughable, but what he found worse was the fear. Palpable, gut-wrenching, and agonizing. Not fear of the unknown, but fear for who he was leaving behind.

Kennex and his partner, Ari 'Lucky Fox' Barlow, were assigned a job on an abandoned world. They were responding to a distress signal, but all they found was death. The second he set foot on the glassed surface of Diomedes, he should've left. Ari wouldn't have gone easy, but she would have listened if he had been adamant. He could have tried harder.

The last thing Kennex saw was Ari crying. As darkness overtook his senses, there was no peace or rest. Only guilt, horror, and the sinking realization he had failed the only person who had been there for him.

And, because he was not as lucky as Ari, when Kennex died, he didn't get to fade into nothing.

Like a taut, metal wire snapping under pressure, darkness became a blinding white. With a shuddered gasp, Kennex rubbed at his features as his blurry vision cleared.

He wasn't supposed to be here.

Gone was the dreary landscape of Diomedes. In its place were hills of rolling, white grain and clear blue sky. He stood on a dirt path that cut through the field as far as he could see, and the shadowy outline of a city rose from the horizon.

Kennex turned to speak to his partner, always by his side, but he was alone.

"Ari?" A prickling sensation spread through his chest as the hair on the back of his neck stood on end. Thunder rumbled behind him—faint and foreboding.

"Kennex."

The wind whispered, bringing a wave of unease. Kennex's mouth went dry, and his shallow breaths brought no relief. He was choking. His heart pounded behind his ribs. Every beat a bruising punch.

"He belongs to Aether now."

Kennex flinched at the crack of lighting, and it triggered a painful recollection. He clutched at his chest and glanced down. Gold. Shimmering, yet sinister. It soaked his shirt, poured from the gaping hole where his heart should be, and painted his fingers in the radiant shade.

"Kennex!"

He spun at his partner's desperate cry but found only a thick forest shrouded in darkness. Smooth, white bark trees with vibrant, red leaves blocked his view. A dark fog seemed trapped behind the tree line and peering into the void was fruitless. Ari's voice screamed from somewhere in the depths.

"Ari?" Kennex sprinted to a gap between the trees, but he slammed into an unseen wall. He couldn't cross through. He tried again to no avail. With a frustrated, guttural cry, Kennex slammed his fists into the invisible force blocking him from Ari.

She was in danger. He remembered now. X'ael arrived like an omen to the end. The immortal had taken from him, and Kennex knew he would take from Ari as well.

"You are going to hurt yourself, Kennex," a Khareesian accented voice said. The formal tone was recognizable, and Kennex glanced over his shoulder to see Lain only a few feet behind him. The medic's dark skin was a sharp contrast to the white field he stood in. Kennex didn't understand how Lain found them, but it was a relief.

"Lain." Kennex marched to him and pointed to the forest. "Ari is trapped. We gotta get to her. She was hurt, *bad*. An infusion—"

"She isn't yours to worry about anymore," Lain cut him off. Kennex's panic shifted to distrust as his frown deepened. Something about Lain's glowing gold eyes were wrong. Not the color, but an unsettling depth existed that hadn't been there before. "Ari is gone."

"No. She's not," Kennex snapped. "She's right *fraking* there! Help me get to her." Lain tilted his head, and Kennex felt small under his gaze. With a pained whisper, he shook his head. "You're not Lain. Who are you?"

The doppelganger took one step forward, and Kennex took one back. Its lips curled up, and Kennex noted there were too many teeth in the broad smile.

"I am what you need me to be," it replied. "A reflection of your desire."

"Then make yourself useful and help me save her."

Kennex turned back to the forest. Unsettled or not, Ari was waiting. She needed him.

A hot breath fanned against the back of his neck. Kennex tensed as the words, still spoken in Lain's voice, pierced through him. "She is *gone*. She is beyond your reach. This is not where you will save her." Arms wrapped around him—his torso, his neck, his hips, his shoulders. Too many to be the Khareesian. He was dragged away from the forest in a tangle of limbs. "Fate has deemed this to be where your paths diverge. There is no going back now."

Kennex screamed, but an arm wrapped over his mouth and dragged him down.

His stomach lurched, wind whipping past him, but he never hit the ground.

He fell through it.

- TWO -

Kennex woke with a sinking sensation he couldn't quite grasp.

Nausea rolled over him as he laid flat in a bed that was too soft to be his. He shifted to the side only to dry heave. No relief came from the action, and Kennex was left with a pit in his gut and the gnawing panic that something was very wrong.

Ari's screams rang in his ears.

A glass of water, held by an unfamiliar hand, interrupted his view of the tan tiled floors. On instinct, Kennex grabbed the wrist of the person holding it. The glass shattered on the ground, and a squeak silenced the ringing in his ears. The wrist he held belonged to a petite woman. Her light green eyes were blown wide, and the emotion was clear. Surprise. Fear. Light blonde hair fell past her shoulders in loose curls.

"You're okay," she murmured in a voice as soft as the color scheme overwhelming him. Pastel shades on and around her. Walls of pale green and blue, glass faced cabinets filled with medical supplies, and off-white curtains separating each cot. As if those clues weren't enough, the breezy dress she wore was layered in folds of white. *Medic.* Kennex was in a medbay. "Everything is okay."

He shook his head. She was wrong. His eyes dragged over the room. The four other cots were empty, and a window sat on the wall across from him. The glass was engraved in frosted, swirling designs that allowed rays of Sol to pass through in glittering patterns that decorated the floor. The frame was cracked open. A breeze flittered in, rippling the sheer white curtains on either side. He stiffened. Not a medbay. A clinic.

Kennex was world bound.

The medic tried to pull away, but he tightened his grip on the pale wrist. His attention snapped back to her. She gulped, and her bounding pulse raced under his palm. Kennex tugged her closer. "Where the hells am I?"

"Sir, please calm—"

"Where is Ari?" Kennex asked the only question that mattered. The memory of her blood haunted him. His gear was gone, replaced with tan canvas material, and his skin was clean. All of it, signs that time had passed, and it was unnerving. When the medic didn't reply, he shook her. "Where is—"

"I don't know!" The medic exclaimed. "I don't know who that is!"

Anger flared, near blinding. Kennex sucked in a deep breath and forced himself to push it down. Smother the heat of his rage, swallow the sharp bite of his fear, and focus. Kennex loosened his grip on the woman and spoke as steady as he was able.

"I'm sorry. My name is Kennex. What is yours?"

Her eyes darted down to their hands, and he hesitated before releasing her. She clutched her wrist against her chest and took in a shaky breath of her own. "I'm Lyris."

"Lyris," Kennex repeated. "Lyris, *please*."

Lyris shook her head. "Let me go get someone. I'll be back."

She tried to leave. Unsatisfied, Kennex jumped up from the bed to follow but hissed when a stinging, penetrating pain rocketed up through his heel. He lifted his foot to find a glass shard buried in the flesh of his sole. He pulled the glass out, but no blood dripped from the wound. The glass was clean. A light reflected off the shards littered on the floor.

Slowly, fearfully, Kennex sat down and raised his ankle to rest on his knee. His fingers found gold. The inch long, shallow wound glittered. He rubbed his thumb against it. The pain faded.

"You're Ascendant."

Kennex startled. He looked up from his wound to see the medic had stayed. "No." He snapped. "No, I'm not."

"You are now," Lyris whispered.

The wound was already halfway closed. Remembering the degree of his injury on Diomedes, Kennex let his foot fall and reached back for his collar. Lyris spoke up, but he ignored her to pull his shirt off.

Just like Ari, Kennex had his own collection of scars. His most prominent and memorable existed on his abdomen. A curved indent of discolored skin, from his left hip to just under his right ribcage, where his mother attempted to gut him—supposedly, for his own good. Another scar, less prominent but equally as memorable, were four raking lines across his right ribcage courtesy of Recluse's talons. Kennex had lunged between the Dracck and Ari during one of the first punishments the monster of a man dealt to her. Ari had been furious at the interruption. Furious he had gotten himself clawed for her. It had been one of their most heated arguments.

New to him, were the scars overlying his heart.

Perhaps calling them scars was inaccurate. Kennex touched the glowing skin. The texture of a scar hid at the center of the radiating golden hues. The spattering of new color on his chest was chaotic. A large mass of it over his heart with lines and smaller splotches trailing down to his belly. If he closed his eyes, he could picture the mess of metal and tissue this area had been.

"How?" Kennex breathed.

"I don't know. Nobody does." Lyris replied to the question he had directed more to the universe than to her. "You've been the hot topic for the last nine days." Lyris continued to talk, ramble, but her voice fell out of focus. Kennex stared at her blankly. He knew time had passed, but he had hoped it would've been a day at most. He stood again. "Kennex?"

He didn't stop when glass pressed into his feet. Lyris called after him, but Kennex scrambled to the door.

Oh, Aether. Ari. His last memories were of her bleeding out, struggling as his lights went dark. Ari was left to fend for herself against Ascendant X'ael on the dead planet of Diomedes.

Kennex barreled out the building and blinked rapidly as Sol's rays blinded him. He didn't stop as his eyesight adjusted. He stumbled down a white stone path lined with gray and yellow flowers. The tan brick, white roofed buildings matched the one he rushed out of. Others on the path leapt out of his way. Yarians. They were all Yarians. Voices called after him, and he only paused when he reached a fork in the path. Kennex scanned the space, and he got stuck in the sky. It was void of any clouds, but a large mass of metal interrupted the color. It was perpendicular to the horizon in an overhead arch. A ring around the world. There were buildings and movement on the interior of it. The sight was a damning clue to his location, but the impossible nature of it stunned him.

Illyarium.

Third world from Sol, but center of the universe.

A longing for Ari's presence ached in his chest. What he wouldn't give to have her muttering an untimely joke about this situation.

"Kennex Hall."

The voice did not belong to Lyris. Female but raspier. Kennex tore his gaze away from the ring and turned. Lyris was there, but beside her was an Ascendant. Kennex had seen her face broadcasted before. This immortal was a fan favorite.

"Come back with us before you hurt yourself," Ascendant Vira ordered.

"I can't hurt myself anymore."

"Then before you hurt someone else," Vira responded with ease. "We need to talk."

"Where is Ari?" Kennex gasped. His desperation overpowered any sense of calm he had. Kennex's reputation labeled him levelheaded. He wielded logic as often as his hand cannon. However, Kennex was frayed at the edges. He was free falling, swinging for something to grasp, but only finding air. The anger he had quelled broke free. "Where the *frak* is Ari Barlow!?"

"Gone."

A new voice joined the conversation, but it was not new to him. Vira cursed but it was muted in comparison to the tune being whistled. Kennex looked over his shoulder to see X'ael. Just as he did on Diomedes, the Ascendant swaggered to the scene. His black cloak swayed with each step and light glinted off his bronze armor. The Yarians on the path knelt as he passed.

"What?" Kennex breathed as his body turned. Vira called out his name, but it was fading background noise to him. He stumbled forward a step. "What did you just say?"

X'ael tilted his head, only a few feet away now, and amusement of all emotions filled his red eyes. "I said she was gone, Ascendant Hall."

"Don't *fraking* call me that." Kennex said. "What did you do to her?"

"Nothing." X'ael shrugged. "I only allowed fate to follow its course. Death had come for her, Ascendant. It had come for you both. Only you were strong enough to survive." Kennex shook his head. "Aether deemed you worthy of a second chance."

"No." Kennex's heart raced, panic suffocated him, and he gaped. "No, no. You're lying. Where is she? Where is Ari?"

X'ael lifted his hand, palm up, and a glimmer of gold appeared out of thin air to fall in his waiting hold. The Ascendant tossed it to Kennex who caught it on instinct. He didn't need to look at what he was holding to know what it was. Kennex recognized the weight and the raised angles of the charm pressing against his palm. He opened his hand to stare at Ari's necklace. Flecks of dried blood clung to the metal.

"Her Meraki," X'ael said. Kennex stiffened at the word—the final symbol of passing. A token of a loved one lost. "If it gives you peace, her last words were of you."

In a blink, Kennex lunged for the Ascendant who took his life. X'ael grunted as they hit the ground. Straddling the immortal, Kennex pounded his fist into X'ael's face. *Again and again and again.* He felt his knuckles tear, the satisfying crunch of X'ael's nose and cheek crushing in, but the lack of blood only fueled his rage. Light blinded Kennex as it shone from X'ael's unrecognizable features, and the immortal had the audacity to laugh. Through the punches, the cackling sound filled Kennex's heart with a new level of hatred.

The harder he hit, the louder X'ael laughed.

Cold hands grasped either side of Kennex's face from behind, and, with one snap to the left, Kennex's world went dark.

- THREE -

Kennex was dizzy from waking in places he did not recognize.

He stood on a set of black, stone steps that led up to a tall arch. Red moss grew over sections of the stone entrance. Behind him a field of grain. At the foot of the stairs began a dirt path that cut through the field and led to the forest of white trees with bloody leaves.

Kennex took a step down, onto the path, but the shaking sound of ice being mixed into a drink drifted from the stone structure he had turned from. He hesitated, only for a second, before climbing back up the stairs and through the stone arch.

It was hard to pinpoint the sound, it echoed off the surrounding stone, but it grew louder as he ventured deeper into the structure through a hallway of tall arches. In the spaces between each pillar were gardens of overgrowing plants in various shades of red. Vines crawled up the stones, a contrast to the black, and overhead was a bright glare. To his left, the shaking of ice against metal was replaced with liquid being poured into a glass.

"You died. Again." Trig scoffed. She stood behind the remains of a wall, as if she were working behind the bar at the Barrel. "That was quick. I expect that kind of screwhead move from Ari. Not you."

The tattoos on her brown skin were the right shade of green but they spun too fast and in a pattern that seemed to change into something new every second. She had the right number of teeth, but her hand, resting on the stone between them, had three extra fingers.

"You're not Trig."

"I'm close enough. Aren't I?" The mimic shrugged.

"Leave me alone," Kennex snapped. His plans to leave vanished as his path and the entrance he originally came through disappeared. Instead, he stood in a circular space where five endless stone arched halls branched away from him.

"Whether you know it or not, you want me here, Kennex."

No argument filled his mind, he mumbled, "Where exactly is here?"

"That's not a simple answer."

Kennex glared at the mimic who mixed another imaginary drink. "I'll take any answer right now."

"All right," the mimic hummed, "Joon."

"Joon?" He didn't recognize the word.

"Yes. It's Diomedes' capital city." The mimic grinned, and Kennex hated that the familiar sight of Trig's excitement automatically placed him at ease. "Diomedes was a special place. Did you know it was united? The entire planet fell under one democracy that was housed here within these very walls." It paused in its bartending imitations. "While other worlds had leaders that squabbled for control of land or invisible borders, the government here was at peace. A true utopia."

Kennex studied the aged stone and overgrowing gardens with new understanding. "For a utopia, it seems to have failed."

"No. Not failed. Destroyed."

"The story of Aether and Erebus battling here..."

"It's true." The mimic nodded. A deep, ancient melancholy filled Trig's eyes. One he had never seen in the real bartender. "This was where it all ended—where the greatest sacrifice was made, yet it lives on as a whispered rumor."

Though time had passed, it felt like only a moment ago he had been walking side by side with Ari regaling this very story. Arguing with his partner over the possible sacrifice was very different than standing in the aftermath of it. A new weight existed when the mimic told the tale.

Kennex began to understand Ari's view on the matter when she blamed Aether for the carnage.

"Ari was half right," the mimic said. Kennex tensed at the response to his internal monologue. "It *was* Aether. He was the one who killed this planet. It was this world or the entire universe. Every man, woman, and child that perished are heroes. The universe owes them for choosing to become a part of something larger."

"The story didn't make it sound like much of a choice."

The mimic chuckled and leaned forward on the makeshift bar between them. "Those are Ari's feelings, not yours, Kennex."

"Stop talking as if you were there with us." Kennex snapped. His hand slammed down on the stone as he squared up with the creature.

"I was there." It shrugged. "Retroactively. I've seen the memory. I see *all* your memories." The mimic began to shake the imaginary tumbler once more. Among the noise of shaking ice was the soft sound of fingers tapping against a metal counter. The mimic looked away from Kennex and grinned. "What? You need another already?"

"Trig, I don't pay you to judge me." Ari's voice responded.

Kennex looked to his right to see her sitting in her usual spot by his side. She was half slumped over with bruises littering the side of her face. One eye was swollen closed, and her short brown hair was messily pulled up as much as it could be. Kennex remembered this. It happened only a few months ago.

"You don't pay me at all, idiot."

"Are you this rude to all your customers?" The memory of Ari countered. *"Keep it up, and I'll take my business elsewhere."*

The mimic chuckled, just as Trig had. "As if any other bartender on this port would put up with you."

Ari turned to face him and Kennex sucked in a sharp breath. The memory of her waved at him. *"Hello? Your partner is being brutally abused here."* Kennex lifted his hand to her. *"Mind stepping in before—"*

Her words and image dispersed in a mist the moment his fingers made contact. As she disappeared, Kennex's throat tightened, and his stomach churned. He knew it was only a memory but the loss stung all the same.

"You were chosen, Kennex, and that means we now exist as one."

"What does that even mean?" Kennex's voice came out a raspy croak.

"Your resurrection was not a coincidence or lucky break." Kennex stared at the spot Ari briefly existed, but a cold hand grabbed his chin and forced his gaze forward. The mimic was leaning over the bar as it held him in a vice grip. Kennex tried to break free. The fingers of the creature elongated and tangled behind his head in his hair. "Your resurrection was an *opportunity*." The fingers stretched until they wrapped the circumference of his head. "Do not let it go to waste."

The fingers squeezed until, with a pop, Kennex's vision went black.

- FOUR -

The bed Kennex laid in was softer than the last. Arguably, too soft. As he blinked away his disorientation, a cozy bedroom appeared. Dark blue walls with splashes of color painted in a haphazard manner. The desk to the side was overflowing with books, papers, and a few tablets. Closer than the desk was a bedside table. On it rested a familiar gold necklace. Kennex snatched it off the surface and sat up.

"Welcome back to the world of the living."

Beyond the foot of the bed, Vira glared at him. The orange tint of her glasses did nothing to hide the irritation in her pale blue eyes. Her chair was twisted so she could cross and rest her arms on the back.

Kennex closed his fingers around the necklace. "You killed me."

"Yeah. I did," Vira replied. "You were beating the scrap out of X'ael on the streets in front of a group of adherents. You left me with no choice."

"Why didn't I come back to life there?" Kennex asked. He didn't have a significant amount of experience dealing with Ascendants, but he was under the impression their resurrections were near immediate.

"You did." Vira replied. "But you stayed unconscious. It takes a bit before your body adjusts to the shock of coming back to life. After you die some more, you won't lose consciousness."

Kennex scoffed. *Of course. Dying just takes practice.* He looked away from her.

"I wanted to drag you back to the clinic and cuff you to the bed, but Lyris thought you'd do better in a more comfortable setting."

"Where are we?"

"Her home."

Kennex tried to climb out of bed, but Vira stood and stalked around to stop him.

"You hardly deserve the comfort, but Lyris has always been too kind," she snipped. Kennex furrowed his brow. "Don't think I didn't see the mark you left on her." Confusion was interrupted by the memory of his hand wrapped around her wrist. He didn't think he held on tight enough to leave evidence. "The next time you even think of leaving her bruised—"

"That wasn't my intention."

"*I don't care,*" Vira snarled. "I'll—"

Kennex blew out an annoyed breath, "Kill me?"

"You have a lot to learn, new light." Vira spoke slowly. The anger in her voice becoming measured and controlled. "And I will happily teach you the first lesson." Kennex involuntarily stiffened at the clear threat. "There are fates worse than death."

Kennex didn't understand the sentiment, but he had bigger worries than pissing off the Ascendant in front of him. He rose from the bed, and Vira, who was his height, didn't cower or flinch. "Look, I'm sorry. I never meant to hurt the medic. I'm just trying to figure out what's going on."

Finding answers was the first step in getting the hells out of here.

"So is everyone else." Vira crossed her arms.

"What do you mean?"

"How often do you think we have a situation like this, new light?"

Kennex bristled, at her tone or the nickname he wasn't sure. It never occurred to him that his status would be a mystery to the Ascendants as well. His thoughts lingered on the mimic in his brain.

"Do you know something?" Vira commented. Kennex's eyes snapped back to hers and irritation had melted into intrigue. He stepped past her but paused by a mirror propped up in the corner. "Tell me, new light."

Kennex shook his head. "Don't call me that."

"It's a term of endearment for new Ascendants."

"Not the way you say it," Kennex muttered. He unlatched the clasp on Ari's necklace to string around his neck, but his eye caught the polished metal of a silver link among the gold. "The chain broke. Who fixed it?"

Vira stepped closer and spoke over his shoulder, "The medic you attacked." Kennex huffed. Guilt lingered only for a second. He hadn't meant to cause harm, especially to the only non-Ascendant he had met thus far, but it wasn't as if he could take that back. "Now, what do you know, *new light*?" She spat the nickname out with more disdain than before.

Kennex turned to meet her gaze head on, and he shook his head. "I know I need to get out of here. Where can I find a ship?"

"Do you actually think I'd tell you?"

Kennex locked his jaw and left. Across the room, he pushed through the split in the middle of a thick curtain hanging from the doorframe and stepped into a living space that was only a bit larger than where he came from. The walls and décor matched what he woke to, but the room consisted of a small couch aimed toward an aged holoscreen built into the wall and a kitchen area. Lyris was mixing something in a bowl when he stepped out, but she froze at his entrance.

"Oh, good morning." Lyris brushed her hands off before wiping them on her patchwork apron. The medic uniform had been traded for a plain, pink dress with long sleeves rolled up to her elbows. "How do you feel?"

"I'm fine," Kennex replied curtly. More lie than truth, but none of his problems could be fixed by a routine medic. "Where can I find a ship?" Lyris' gaze snapped over his shoulder as Vira entered the room behind him. He huffed. "Never mind. I'll find it myself."

"You really think wandering around the Court of Aether in your pajamas is the answer?" Vira asked.

Kennex stiffened. "The Court of—I'm in the Court of Aether?"

"Where else did you think you'd be?" Vira scoffed. He didn't have an answer. The ring in the sky revealed he was on Illyarium, and he probably should have assumed he'd be in the court. It made sense, but his mind hadn't connected the dots until now.

A touch settled on the side of his arm, and Kennex startled. Lyris offered a soft smile, "Would you like some water?"

Her hand rested on his bicep, and he noticed a bruise forming around her wrist. Kennex swallowed and nodded.

She directed him toward a two-person table off to the side and he fell into the seat. Vira followed and leaned against a nearby counter—her glare never falling from him. Lyris returned with water, as promised, and she handed it to him before settling in the other seat.

"Thank you," Kennex responded. He lifted the glass but hesitated. "And I'm sorry. For hurting you. That was never my intention."

Lyris' face tinted red, and she pulled her sleeves down. "Please, it's fine. You were confused and scared and—Don't worry yourself over this. Honestly, I've had worse." Vira let out a scoff that the medic ignored. "Did you rest well?"

Kennex thought of the nightmare that plagued him after death and lied. "Yes. Thank you."

"I know waking in a clinic can be stressful. I hoped this would be less jarring."

Kennex downed the water then pushed to stand. "I'd like to be out of your hair as soon as possible. If you'd—"

"We're not telling you where the nearest shipyard is, new light."

"Why not?" Kennex snapped. He returned Vira's glare with gusto. "Why do you care if I leave?"

Vira crossed her arms. "Because you haven't seen Malachi yet." Kennex recognized the rarely used name of the Curator. "In fact, now that you're awake I'll take you to him," Vira mockingly added, "Get you out of our hair."

Rather than argue, Kennex nodded. Meeting with the Curator was not high on his list of desires, but getting off this planet might be easier if he followed the path of least resistance. The longer he thought on it, the more his curiosity was piqued.

"Wait! Let me get you some clothes to change into." Lyris motioned for him to follow, and, after a beat of continued glaring between him and Vira, he did. She was in the bedroom rustling through a drawer. "You can borrow some of my husband's clothes. You're taller than him, but I don't think it'll make much of a difference."

Kennex nodded as she handed him a stack of items and left the room. For a moment, all he could do was stare at a spot on the wall. Being on Illyarium was painful for many reasons. Kennex had dreamed of escaping the Port of Acheron—escaping Recluse. Realistically, if his dream came to fruition, it would have been a run-down house on a no name colony or poverty out in Wild Space. That would have been enough. Ari and him would have survived. They always did.

If Kennex were being honest with himself, if given the freedom of hope, his true dream would have looked like this—a small house on a safe, well supplied world, somewhere where he didn't have to make sacrifices.

This was a devastating derision of that dream.

Illyarium was never a world he seriously considered settling on. It was laughable to go from nothing in Acheron to calling a capital world in Inner Orbit home. Dreams rarely followed sense or logic though. While all of this should have been a gift, Kennex didn't stand here as a man who had escaped on his own free will. He was trapped. Recluse's grimy grip traded for a gilded cage. Worse, the person who was by his side in every iteration of his dream was not here.

The universe had never been very kind to him, but this was a new level of cruel.

"Stop squirming. You're like a child," Vira scolded as they walked.

Kennex tried again to adjust the pants Lyris lent him. She claimed her husband wasn't *much* shorter than him, but his exposed ankles said otherwise. Kennex was beginning to think he should have stayed in what he had before. Luckily, the jacket fit. It didn't hold a flame to the weighted leather of his own that he prayed wasn't left abandoned on Diomedes. He attempted to tug the pants down. "I'm not squirming."

They walked on a path that cut through an area of one-story buildings. It was plain and simple. Nothing about it screamed 'Court of Aether.' He had seen fancier colonies.

"This is really the court?"

"Yes, but we're in the village."

"Village?"

"The Adherent Village." Vira nodded. Kennex had heard of adherents, but up until now he was convinced they were a myth. Adherents dedicated their lives to work in the Court of Aether. They willingly chose to throw away freedom to service Ascendants and acolytes. A truly deranged concept, in his opinion. "Ascendants have no need for a clinic which is why we brought you here after you arrived."

Kennex glanced at the faces staring at them. "This is the only clinic in the entire court?"

"Well, there is one for acolytes, but neither X'ael nor I had any interest in visiting there."

"You'd do well not speaking that bastard's name to me." Kennex snapped. Vira chuckled and it irritated him more. "What?"

"Nothing." Vira shook her head with a muted laugh. "Hearing someone call him a bastard is just funny." Kennex opened his mouth to speak, but she cut him off. "To me, bastard has different connotations."

"What would you refer to him as?"

"A sniveling weasel. The Curator's whore." Vira laughed again. "He's more annoying than he is dangerous." Kennex locked his jaw as his hands curled into fists. Annoying was not the word that came to mind when X'ael shot him. "But I understand your interaction with him was...*tense*. I am sorry about what he did to your partner."

Kennex shook his head. "X'ael didn't kill Ari. She isn't dead." Vira shot him a look, clearly pity, but Kennex wasn't delusional. He carried her necklace, her supposed Meraki, but he didn't accept that Ari was dead. Kennex was the logical one, and Ari had been the one with the superior instinct. He was finally beginning to understand what she meant when she made those 'gut calls.' Something deep in him, etched into his very soul, knew Ari was not gone. If she were, part of him would have died with her. "Don't look at me like that."

"I've heard the story. X'ael told us in *excruciating* detail. Your partner was already half dead when he got his hands on her. She fought. She fought like hells, but X'ael reopened every wound she had and left her bleeding to death in a pile," Vira said as if her goal was to share a simple fact, not goad him into anger or hurt him. "It may be best to accept what is."

"You don't know Ari like I do. If you did," Kennex's lips twitched into a small smile that didn't last, "you'd know my partner is too stubborn to die."

Vira chuckled, a response he didn't expect, and nodded. "She sounds fun. It's a shame we got stuck with you rather than her."

Kennex would give anything for the roles to be reversed. For Ari to be immortal and relatively safe in a location like the Court of Aether rather than be injured in Outer Orbit alone and with Recluse breathing down her neck. Besides, the mental image of Ari waking up in this place was comical.

The Ascendants were lucky they ended up with him.

They continued in silence until a new sight greeted him. The path through the village came to an end at a golden gate. The matching fence that stretched out from either side of it made him realize they were in an enclosure. Bile rose in his throat. He couldn't puzzle out if the Ascendants trapping the adherents like this or the adherents choosing this kind of fate disgusted him more.

Vira, who didn't blink twice at the gate, stepped ahead to meet the guard. Kennex assumed he was an Ascendant based on the formal armor and purple cape.

"Open the gates."

"Does the adherent have a work pass for today?"

Vira reached over and grabbed the edge of Kennex's shirt. He startled as she lifted it up to reveal his torso. Stunned, he just stared at her.

"Apologies." The guard opened the gate and Vira let his shirt fall.

Kennex shook his head, "What the actual *frak* is wrong with you?"

"I didn't feel like talking through the situation." Vira shrugged. She walked through and he followed a step behind. "Besides, your shirt is already showing your midriff."

"It is not," Kennex argued and tugged down on the shirt that would most definitely show skin if he lifted his arms.

The second they crossed through the gate, the world changed.

Kennex stumbled as marble and glass surrounded him. For the most part, where they stood was a park. Beautiful patches of greenery were separated by white stone under their feet. Sculptures decorated the area, and, based on the closest one in armor, they were of Ascendants. The few buildings were grand spectacles made of towering marble with accents of gold and glass. The staple, in the distance, was a tower so high it disappeared into the clouds.

"What the hells?" Kennex glanced back to see the gate, but beyond the fenced doors was a matching view. Adherent Village now non-existent. It dawned on him. "It's a net."

"Quick of you to catch on."

Nets were electrical fields used to block off areas from being broached by starships. Designed by a Khareesian engineer, one he couldn't recall the name of but could picture their face from a book back home, nets were used to protect no fly zones. They had also been used in the past to close off certain worlds that were deemed dangerous to the rest of the system. Kennex read nets could project images, but he didn't think it was used in this manner.

"I don't understand."

"Adherents are not worthy to view us without permission. So, to keep the Court of Aether pure, the sight of the Adherent Village is blocked off," Vira responded automatically. Disgust bubbled into anger. Vira shook her head. "Nothing you're about to say I haven't either heard before or argued myself so save it."

Kennex scoffed. "You Ascendants are really okay with Yarians being trapped like that?"

"Some are, some aren't." Vira shrugged. "But technically, the adherents chose that life so there isn't much that can be done."

"They choose to live in a *fraking cage*?"

"You call those bars a cage, but they call it home," Vira replied. "They have a roof over their heads, clothes on their back, food in their bellies, and they are safe. Possibly the safest Yarians in the entire system."

Kennex shook his head and motioned back where they came. "They're *prisoners*."

"Again," Vira glanced at him with a tired resolve, "they put the chains on their own wrists and ankles. It makes arguing for their freedom hard." She nodded once and focused back on their path forward. "You can't save someone who doesn't want to be saved."

Though it left a bitter taste in his mouth, Kennex let the topic fall away. The park had more acolytes than adherents, and the few adherents he did see were in a uniform of all black—their lower faces covered in masks. He tried to focus more on the scenery than the figures they passed. It was how he realized the greenery surrounding them was fake. All of it. Trees, shrubbery, flowers, and grass all held the shine of artificial creation.

Vira led him through the winding park, past a few grand buildings, and right up to the base of the tower. Even this creation was made of white and gold marble which Kennex found to be quite the feat. The entire exterior was smooth with no windows as far as he could see. The only doorway was a lift.

Vira stopped in her tracks, and after a few more steps Kennex stilled as well. He glanced over at her with a raised eyebrow. She simply nodded to the lift. "This is where I leave you."

"You're not coming up?"

"Even if I were allowed, I wouldn't want to," Vira replied. "I have less than no interest in the company you're about to have."

Kennex narrowed his eyes at the statement. He had trouble understanding why an Ascendant of Aether's Light would feel that way toward the man who was their supposed leader.

Vira offered him no other information but nodded toward the lift again. "Go on."

As Kennex approached, the doors automatically opened, and he stepped in warily. The panel wall had only two buttons. Kennex pressed the top one. His gaze met Vira's again.

If Kennex didn't know better, he'd say she looked worried.

"Good luck, new light."

"I said, don't call me that."

The lift doors shut before his complaint had fully left his lips.

- FIVE -

The lift was nothing like the one in Acheron. It was smaller, only able to fit two or three people, and its movements were smooth. The lift was also made entirely of glass. A dim light above allowed him a view of the stone encasing the box. The distance from the ground under his feet increased and watching made him dizzy. Kennex wondered if Ari, who sought out heights but avoided enclosed spaces, would love or hate this.

When the lift slowed to a stop, Kennex rolled his shoulders and steeled himself. His reflection was anxious. If he had his helmet, he wouldn't have to worry about how he looked. He let his eyes focus on the gold charm hanging from his neck and took a steadying breath. The doors slid open.

Kennex was met by another garden. A real one.

Rather than an inner wall, the hallway outside the lift had pillars of white marble cracked with gold veins. At the center was a blossoming garden made up of plants he had never seen before. Not even in books. The flowers seemed unnatural—too many petals, and colors so vibrant they seemed painted. Faceless acolytes tended the garden, but they were robed in dark red not purple. The bubbling of flowing water, the chimes of a wordless song, and the too sweet smell of the flowers should've put him at ease. Every aspect designed to create a calming effect, but Kennex's heart was racing in his chest.

"Ascendant."

Kennex startled. To his left, three purple robed acolytes approached. The one in the center wore ornate, golden chains and his otherwise white mask was decorated in matching, shimmering lines. He snorted. What Acolyte Rozick wouldn't give to have those adornments.

"Ascendant," the center acolyte repeated.

"Don't call me that."

"The Curator is awaiting your presence. We have been tasked with fetching you."

Kennex resisted the instinct to bolt for the lift.

They led him down the monotonous curved hall to an open stone arch against the outer wall. The two plain acolytes took their places on either side as the lead ascended the dimly lit, winding stairs beyond it. Kennex followed him up a few dozen steps until they reached a double door of dark wood. Like the rest of this space, it felt ancient. Moss had seeped into wood, giving the air a damp, aged smell, and swirling patterns were burned into it. The acolyte stopped and bowed his head.

With a huff, Kennex pushed through the heavy door.

Light blinded him, and Kennex raised an arm to try and block Sol's glare. The door led out onto a large, circular balcony. A stone railing wrapped around the space, allowing a view of the world around them. From here, Kennex could see more than just the Overflow Ring. He could see the edge of the Golden Halo. Whereas the Overflow Ring was stationary with connections that tethered it in place, the Golden Halo changed location as it spun. Right now, it sat parallel to the horizon, Sol's rays glinting off it made the sky glow—an artificial sunset.

Furniture decorated the balcony. The first sight of modern technology since the lift. A curved desk with a holotop sat to his right, bookshelves lined the railing behind it, and a couch sat on the other side of the balcony to his left. At the center, was a world map of Illyarium. The planet was being projected from the small, circular screen implanted into the floor. It rotated slowly in front of him. Kennex took a step, and the world map flickered into a broader view of the entire Meridian System. This map was wider than it was high, and it allowed Kennex to see the man standing behind it.

The Curator.

Kennex had seen the religious figure on news channels and broadcasted sermons but seeing him in person was a unique experience. His stark white suit was spotless. The material as rich as the acolytes' robes and decorated with gold chains and jewelry. Medals were pinned to his chest, and Kennex couldn't think of a single feat that deserved such accolades. The Curator's helmet was infamous—soft white, shaped with a crown on top, and radiant gold glass hiding his face.

"Welcome, Kennex Hall," the Curator greeted. His voice was quiet and calm. Kennex almost wanted to use the word soothing, but it hardly fit the man. "I have been awaiting your arrival."

At all times, Kennex carried a mental list of complaints and insults he'd spew at the Curator if ever given the chance. A trivial thing he never thought he'd have the opportunity to use. However, with the Curator stalking toward him, Kennex found himself speechless.

The head priest was taller than him with broad shoulders. It didn't match the image he expected. Kennex stood his ground. He had faced beasts and men far worse than the religious bastard that stood before him.

"X'ael has told me much about you," the Curator hummed. A hand lifted toward his face and Kennex realized the Curator wore white gloves with gaudy rings over it. The ring around the middle of his right thumb created a sharp talon. The Curator pressed the tip along the side of Kennex's face. A pinch, as his skin broke under the talon, and he scrunched his nose as a trail of pain followed the drag of the Curator's thumb. Kennex didn't let his gaze waver. Unable to see the Curator's eyes, he focused on the light reflecting off the man's helmet where the cut on his cheek shimmered. "So very interesting."

Kennex hated himself. He had questions to ask, accusations to throw, hatred to spew, but all the words collided into a jumbled mess at the back of his throat. Ari always had something to say. This was never a problem she ran into, and he wished he had an ounce of her bold audacity.

"Speak your mind, Ascendant Hall," the Curator chuckled.

"Don't call me that," he snarled, finally finding his voice. "Why the hells am I here?"

"Is it not obvious? You were reborn, so X'ael brought you home."

"This is *not* my home."

The Curator turned his back to Kennex and wandered to the map of the Meridian System. Kennex took the nonchalance as the insult it was. "Kennex, I hesitate to express this to you, because I know you'll only argue further, but the truth is," the Curator lifted a hand and motioned for him to follow with two fingers, "this was always fated to be your home."

Confused, Kennex stumbled forward. "That's nonsense. Just like the rest of the scrap you preach."

"Oh, my little lost one." The Curator chuckled. Kennex was surprised to find a nickname he hated worse than 'new light.' "Your eyes have finally been opened, and it is overwhelming to be thrust into such a grand truth, but the universe is so much larger than the tiny kingdom Recluse reigns over in Outer Orbit."

Kennex stiffened at the mention of his boss. "You don't know—"

"I know more than you want me to," he sighed, turning to face him. "Kennex Hall. Born in an unnamed port to a woman without a credit to her name. Your father was a stranger to your mother, and she was all you ever knew. The two of you migrated to the Port of Acheron. At eleven, she attempted to kill you. I am sorry about that."

Kennex was off-balanced, and the lightheaded sensation overwhelming him wasn't from the thin air.

"You met your partner, Arienna Barlow, not long after, and the two of you remained on the port. You found work with the criminal boss there. Climbed from messengers to ring fighters to skilled task runners. You earned names for yourselves—Lucky Fox and Venom. It is quite the accomplishment." The Curator spoke like a proud father. No judgment, only admiration, and it left Kennex reeling. "Unfortunately, with an employer like Recluse there really is no happy end or prospect for a greater life."

"How the hells do you know that? That's not something you can just find in an enforcer's record or bounty placard."

"I make it my mission to know my children, Kennex," he responded, and Kennex scoffed at the claim. "The moment you were blessed with the light, you were ushered under my wing. Yes, your birth was an unusual one, but I love you all the same."

Kennex pointed at the Curator. "You're out of your *fraking* mind."

Done with this conversation, and too confused to lay into the man, he turned on his heel.

Kennex was halfway to the doors when the Curator called out, "Ari is alive."

His chest ached as his feet stumbled. The only string of Illyarian words that could bring him to a crashing halt. Kennex glanced over his shoulder to find the Curator watching. His hands clasped behind him.

"Your faith in her is well deserved. She is an incredible young woman."

"How do you know?" Kennex stormed back. He had been confident in his partner's survival, but hearing it aloud was different. His voice cracked, "How do you know that for sure? Where is she?"

The Curator tilted his head. "I don't know where she is, but I know she is alive. The Ascendants I routed to Diomedes found no sign of her or the child."

"You sent Ascendants to get her?" Kennex furrowed his brow.

"Of course," the Curator blurted. "No being deserves to have their corpse left in the open like that. Once I knew of your existence, I knew you'd want her put to rest properly." He shook his head. "I even had them try to trace the shuttle that had left Diomedes, but they came to a dead end. My Ascendants found no corpse, only an unhelpful medic on Kairon who claimed Ari was no longer in the region."

Lain. Kennex wasn't quite sure how Ari managed to get herself to Kairon as injured as she was, but he had learned long ago not to doubt her.

"But," the Curator continued, "just because she is alive does not mean she isn't in danger."

Kennex snapped back to the moment. "What does that mean?"

"The child."

"The one your acolytes were trying to kill?" Kennex snorted. "I knew you zealots were insane, but that was beyond what I thought you people were capable of."

The Curator held his hands up. "Please. You do not understand. Do you truly think I would send my acolytes and a literal child to the edge of the system with the mission of death for no reason?"

"Yeah. I do."

The Curator pressed on, "My suspicion is your partner is with this child, and, as long as they are together, Ari will be in *immense* danger."

Nothing about the job on Diomedes had been normal—the kid included. Death was associated with her existence. The body count was eight—nine if he included himself. Even on her own, Ari was a walking, talking danger magnet. It came for her every single day.

"Kennex—"

"Stop using my name like that."

The Curator chuckled, "You do not like me calling you Ascendant nor a term of endearment. How else can I refer to you?" Kennex felt like the religious leader had his fingers buried in his mind—worming through his white matter and plucking out parts of his identity. "This situation is a puzzle you are trying desperately to put together. I see it on your face. But, you do not have all the pieces, and until you do this is not something you will ever be able to grasp."

"Then give me the pieces," Kennex demanded.

"You and I both know that would do no good," the Curator hummed. "Would you believe anything I offered you?" Kennex was annoyed at such an accurate assessment. His natural inclination was to argue with anything the Curator claimed. "Exactly. So, instead, I will offer you a word."

Kennex crossed his arms and tried to ignore how the edge of his shirt rose. "A word?"

"A word. There's power in words. Even more power in knowledge. You know this," he responded. Again, the religious icon was telling him what Kennex did and did not know, and again, he was right. "*See-ames.*"

"Excuse me?"

"*See-ames,*" the Curator repeated. A hiss in the word made Kennex suspect it was Otri.

Kennex tilted his head with a scoff. "Can I request an Illyarian word?"

"Oh," the Curator chuckled and turned back to the map. "That would be too easy for you, Kennex, and you're a fan of the hunt." Kennex locked his jaw. "You may leave now. I will notify Ascendant Vira to be your guide here in the court."

The Curator had diverted his attention away. His hands were typing in the air—the display hidden behind the glass of his helmet. Kennex glanced at the exit then back to the man.

"How do you know I won't escape?" Kennex asked.

"Escape? That word insinuates we're holding you captive." The Curator lifted a hand without looking over his shoulder. "You have full permission to come and go as you please. You are an Ascendant and have all the rights of one."

"Fine. How do you know I won't just leave?"

"Because, Kennex," he could picture the smug smile heard in the Curator's voice, "you would never leave your partner in danger."

The silence was painful, and Kennex wasn't quite sure how long he stood there staring at the Curator's back before leaving.

- SIX -

Long term, Kennex's goal would be finding the nearest shipyard to charter—or steal—a starship and find Ari. Short term, he needed answers. Rushing into a fight without the proper information made his skin crawl. Kennex wished he had the book about Otradu Ari had stolen for him, but he had never been one to lament over a lack of supply. It was far simpler to just correct the issue.

When the lift brought him back to Illyarium's surface, Vira and Lyris were there waiting for him. The Ascendant leaned back on the elevated base of a statue and the medic stood in front of her. Vira spoke in hushed but pressured words. He couldn't make out what she said, but their stiff stances gave it the air of a disagreement. Vira's eyes lifted from Lyris to land on him, and the conversation abruptly ended. Lyris turned at Vira's distraction, eyes widening.

"Oh, Kennex." Lyris hurried over. Like the other adherents, her breezy dress was solid black, and she wore a matching mask over her lower face. Unlike the others, who sported short sleeves, her arms were covered in black cloth. "How was your meeting with the Curator?"

Kennex wasn't sure how to answer. No part of the meeting had gone like he thought it would. The Curator knew too much about him, and the soft spoken, almost sincere words left him with a sinking pit in his stomach.

"It went well enough that I got assigned to be his babysitter," Vira grunted, the look behind her tinted glasses held boredom.

Ignoring the topic of the meeting, Kennex shook his head. "I need a favor." Vira raised a curious eyebrow, but Lyris nodded without hesitation. "Do you have a console that connects to the yCW? I don't have my vambrace, and there's a few things I have to research."

"Oh, uh, right now? We were instructed—"

"*I* was instructed," Vira cut her off. "*You* should be back in the clinic."

Lyris continued without missing a beat, "*We* were going to show you your housing."

Kennex bit back a scoff of disdain. He had no intentions to stay here long enough to require housing. "I'd prefer to do my research now, if you don't mind."

"Sure." Lyris glanced back at Vira. "Being that we're at court's center, we could go to The Hall of Murals."

"The Hall of Murals?"

"Yes. I know how it sounds, but it's more than just a site for the Ascendant murals." Lyris pointed in the distance, but there was no telling which building she was referencing in the sea of monotonous white and gold. "It's connected to a library."

Kennex perked up. That was better. Finding information about Otri or Stellotrian culture was difficult on the yCW, so few sources commented on the topic, and Otradu was the one capital world in the Meridian System not connected to the web of information.

"All right. The Hall of Murals, it is."

The Hall of Murals would be Ari's nightmare.

It was his first thought as they stepped into the ostentatious building. At the very least, it was aptly named. The front foyer opened into a great hall, longer than it was wide, and at least three stories of walls decorated with murals. These were nothing like the painted illustrations on Acheron.

These murals were a technological wonder.

Each one resembled a painted portrait, but the figures moved in slight ways—a tussling of robes, a twitch of hands around a weapon, a shift in the eyes from one direction to the other. More so, they were changing location every few moments, sliding this way and that, in a blur of light and art.

The Hall of Murals was one of two buildings open to the public, according to Lyris, and it explained the mixed crowds around him. Acolytes and adherents were present, but they mingled with Yarians of various social status based on the clothes he saw. Kennex passed through the masses, that seemed to split for him, to the nearest mural. Closer, he saw the glimmer of holopaneling.

"Huh," Kennex murmured. He had never seen the tech used in such an expansive manner. The mural in front of him was of an immortal he did not recognize. Just like the murals back home though, the Ascendant had a glowing halo behind his head and impressive armor.

Lyris settled beside him. She raised her hand to the screen and tapped on it. The image rippled like disturbed water, and a menu of selections arose. She flipped through the options with memorized ease and the current mural was whisked away, replaced by a familiar face.

"Really?" Vira snorted from behind as they all stared at her mural. Kennex had seen it before. She didn't have one on Acheron, but a small colony world he and Ari had frequented had her on display. Her altars were always overflowing with goods.

In the mural, Vira's brown hair hung around her shoulders in straight curtains rather than the tight bun she wore now. Her armor was bulky and bold in color—a base of dark orange with red and yellow accents. A navy cloak hung off her shoulders. She had no weapon, so her hands rested on her hips. On a loop, the mural's blue eyes would glance down then up again as if sizing up an unseen enemy.

She did not smile.

None of the Ascendants did.

"You look nice," Lyris replied. She motioned to the image with a wave of her hand. "In fact, I think you should wear the cape all the time."

"It's a cloak."

"Mhmm."

Kennex turned away from Vira's mural to glance around, but he was met with hundreds of peering eyes. Attention wasn't new to him. Anytime he and Ari walked through Acheron's market they were watched, but she was typically the focus. Ari was the one people wanted to speak to and draw the notice of. He preferred it that way. Conversation never came as naturally to him as it did to her. Kennex scanned the crowd for danger, an old habit, but found only awe and curiosity. An unsettling reaction he couldn't quite grasp.

"So, uh," he cleared his throat. "There's a mural of every Ascendant here?"

"Not yet." Lyris walked past him. She stopped in the dead center of the hall and pointed overhead. Near the ceiling, the Ascendant's symbol of a winged sword was projected in the air and over it was a glowing number.

974.

"You should have seen the chaos when that number ticked up from 973 last week," Lyris giggled. Kennex's eyes snapped to her in alarm. She shrugged. "I'm not sure how it works, you'd have to ask someone a bit more technologically advanced than me, but it counts all the Ascendants in the Meridian System."

Kennex did not like being included in that count.

"All *active* Ascendants," Vira corrected. "It doesn't count the retired."

"Once they get your mural on the wall, then it'll be complete."

"I don't want to be a mural," Kennex argued.

Vira rolled her eyes. "Yeah, join the club." She glanced around the space and huffed. "Usually, it's only the purple and green cloaks that enjoy the attention."

"What does that mean?" Kennex asked.

"It's rank," Vira explained as she ushered him and Lyris further down the hall. "There are four tiers of Ascendant. The two lowest are indicated by white armor with purple or green cloaks."

Kennex hadn't been aware there was a hierarchy among the immortals.

Guessing his follow up question, Vira added, "The top two tiers are not restricted to a dress code. We can wear whatever armor we prefer. For formal occasions, the cloaks we have are either black or navy. Black being the higher of the two."

Kennex frowned. "X'ael wears black."

"Yeah, I told you he's the Curator's whore," Vira replied.

"Your cape was navy." Kennex purposefully chose the word Vira had argued against, and he heard Lyris giggle under her breath. "You're not at the highest rank?"

"Hells no." Vira pointed to the right when they reached the end of the massive hall as it split in both directions. "Only a handful of people are tier one, and I have no interest in a promotion."

Lyris held up a hand to count on her fingers. "Let's see, you have Ascendant X'ael, Ascendant Nori Tell, Ascendant Leawny Redrow." She hummed. "Ascendant Derrik Russell was in this tier, but he retired." Vira made a soft grunting noise at the comment. "Oh! Ascendant Claren Herring, right?"

Vira nodded. "That's about it at the moment."

"That's not many."

"Tier two has more," Lyris chimed.

Kennex noted the murals were growing sparse as they walked. The end of the hall opened into a new room with tall shelves of books. His quickened pace stuttered when a new sight caught his attention. Off to the side was a normal sized arch that branched away from the main hall.

"Where does that go?" Kennex asked.

Vira led him over. She motioned for him to step in behind her and as he entered the dimly lit space, he recognized more murals. These were different than the others. The colors were gone. Some were painted in shades of gray, others in melancholic blue, and the last group were gold.

"These are the Ascendants out of commission," Vira said. Lyris drifted to the wall, hands clasped in front of her. The space was mostly silent, only hushed conversation, and there were significantly less people. "Gold means they're retired, gray means they're akhylas—"

"Akhylas?"

"Traitor to the light. Ascendants that willingly turned their back to Aether," Vira answered. Kennex didn't know that was an option. "Blue means they're gone."

Another unfamiliar status for an Ascendant. *Gone?* He drifted to a blue mural. The name written on a banner above the Ascendant's head was one Kennex vaguely recognized. He didn't know the Ascendant, but everyone knew the infamous surname. Rames. A blood Ascendant.

"I thought Ascendants couldn't die?" Kennex asked.

Vira stared up at the mural. "We can't." He didn't bother to complain about the inclusion. "But I already told you, new light. Death isn't the worst thing that could happen to you now."

She left, mumbling words to Lyris he didn't catch, but Kennex lingered. Oddly, her sentiment brought him relief. The Ascendants were not infallible beings, and that meant Ari and him may have a shot at pushing back after all.

Knowing he had allowed his curiosity too much control, Kennex focused back on his task. Unfortunately, he had only gotten a few steps out of the dim hall and into the library when he was left in another daze.

"*Aether.*" Kennex breathed in awe. In his lifetime, he had been in one library before on a colony world he couldn't remember the name of. It had been a singular, tiny room filled with a handful of tablets and books in various degrees of care.

The Court of Aether's library didn't seem real. One vast, circular room, taller than it was wide. Multiple levels climbed up with books lining the walls of each ring. Besides shelves, the ground floor was littered with tables and chairs. A few spots even had holo capability.

"What are you looking for?" Lyris asked, breaking him from his spell. "We can request one of the floor scholars to help us find a resource."

"I, uh," Kennex tore his gaze from the view, "I need any books they have on Otradu. One on their language specifically would be helpful."

Vira snorted. "We'll find you a scholar, but I wouldn't hold your breath, new light."

"How many times do I have to tell you not to call me that?"

The Ascendant ignored him as she and Lyris drifted away. Kennex's eyes landed on a nearby holodesk. As he sat down, he glanced over his shoulders waiting to be stopped. He assumed somebody would pull him from this spot and not allow him access, but trouble never came.

Kennex activated the holodesk and searched for information. Not on

Otri, but on his partner. The yCW wouldn't allow him access to bounty placards. Those could only be accessed via physical bounty boards found on settlements around the universe. However, anyone with a record of breaking Illyarian law were marked in the enforcers' database which was accessible to the public.

It took no effort to find Ari.

Lucky Fox's glowing sigil stared back at him from the placard. A familiar sight. What Kennex found unsettling was seeing Ari alone. Up until now, any placard with Lucky Fox also had Venom. They were a problem to the system that came as a pair. The one in front of him, listed for 'terrorism, homicide of eight acolytes, and abduction of a minor', consisted of only her. Kennex hated the sight. He swore he'd always have Ari's back, and this was a distressing reminder of his failure.

Closing out of it, he attempted to find any hint of where a bounty board might be located. Illyarium had bounty sects. XXVI was outsourced from this world, but where they kept their boards was a mystery.

Kennex was desperate to see their status with Recluse. He had faith that Ari slipped the Dracck's grasp, but being out of the temperamental man's hold came with a slew of new dangers. If Kennex were optimistic, he'd cling to the hope that Recluse was keeping this squabble in house. Unfortunately, he knew his ex-employer too well to waste a thought on those chances.

"Kennex." He closed out of the screen and stood. Vira approached with an acolyte in tow. This one was robed in blue. "They have a few books, but we have to follow the scholar."

He nodded in agreement while mentally categorizing this new class of acolyte alongside the gardeners he had seen. The robe colors seemed to coincide with their job whereas adornments announced a hierarchy. They approached a centralized, circular desk with other blue robed acolytes working behind it. The scholar did not speak. She held out a hand to keep them outside the desk which acted as a barrier to the rest of the room. At the very center was a hole, and Kennex realized it was the start of a staircase leading down. The scholar went straight to it and disappeared.

"You got this handled?" Vira asked. "I left Lyris looking at a few books, but I have to check them out for her."

Kennex's eyes widened. "You're gonna just leave me here again? Completely alone?"

"You're a big boy, aren't you, new light?" Vira chuckled before wandering away.

The Curator assigned her as a guide, but Kennex assumed it was a cover. Vira would act as a guard for the religious icon and keep him in check. Anxiety bubbled in his chest as his beliefs fell flat. With no Ascendant watching him, Kennex could just leave. It'd be easy. The building opened to the public, and he could follow the crowd out the door into Sector One. It was the shock that kept him frozen in indecision. As Kennex jumped through mental hoops pondering the nature of the Curator's surely convoluted plan, the scholar returned with an aged chest. She set it in front of him and unlocked it with a metal key.

Inside were three books as old as the chest itself.

"This is it?" Kennex scoffed. "This is all you have on Otradu?" The scholar gave a silent nod. He muttered, "For Aether's sake..."

It was better than nothing but just barely. Kennex grabbed the first book which resembled a journal. Every page filled with handwritten notes in Otri. It wouldn't be helpful without a way to translate. The next book was more official and bound in a black leather. Opening this one, he saw it was a textbook printed in Otri, but there were Illyarian notes written in the margins. That could be useful. The final book was one written in a Khareesian dialect and he was relieved to see a language he could read. This book reminded him of the one he owned back at home.

Kennex flipped through the Khareesian book hoping for an easy answer, but it became clear this venture would not be a quick one.

"You done yet?" Vira called out.

Vira and Lyris had returned to his side. He huffed, "Hardly."

"Aether, it's been an hour, new light. I don't want to spend all day here."

"V, we're in no rush," Lyris said.

"Yes, we are," Vira argued. "I have to get you back to the village."

Kennex closed the book and motioned to them, directing his question to the scholar, "Can I take these?" She gave a curt nod and turned to access a holodesk system a few feet away. Kennex looked up from the interaction to see Vira and Lyris looked equally as surprised. "What?"

"Nothing. Just interesting." Vira made a clicking noise with her mouth. He shook his head, and she added. "Only tier one Ascendants are allowed to rent out the books from the cellar."

Kennex tensed. He only had a second to ponder the insinuation when his line of thought was interrupted. At the same time of Vira suddenly grabbing Lyris, spinning around to protectively hide her, something solid and sharp pierced through his back. Kennex gasped as he stared down at the metal blade protruding from right side of his chest. The sides of it popped out, creating a 'T' shape, and with a harsh tug, Kennex was yanked back. He hit the ground with a strangled gasp as the metal ripped more flesh. The pain was hot and throbbing. His body screamed, but it seemed muted compared to the mind-scrambling fear. He was dying. This would kill him. The thoughts crashed painfully into memories of Diomedes. Kennex blinked up at the too bright, overhead lights. He tried to suck in a strangled gasp, but no air filled his lungs.

Cold, violet eyes glared down at him, but it was the only feature he registered before a boot slammed down on his face.

- SEVEN -

Death was becoming a nuisance.

He had gone twenty-three years without meeting his end only to die three times in the span of what felt like hours. Kennex cursed as he studied the black stone surrounding him. He was growing more familiar with the remains of Joon than he was the Court of Aether.

Standing in the hall of arches, awaiting the mimic to come and plague him, Kennex realized how long he had been apart from Ari. The thought barreled into him. There were a few times where jobs would pull them apart, but they avoided those best they could. The longest stint without one another had been three days.

At least for Kennex, the bulk of her absence had been while he was asleep in cryo.

Ari was dealing with the days as they came.

He worried she'd slip into her more self-destructive habits without him there.

Kennex touched a red vine that hung low from where it was plastered on the arch above. It dissolved in his grasp and left his fingers painted red. Kennex brushed his hand off, casting the red dust into the air, when a scuffle came from behind. He turned, expecting the mimic, but found Ari.

Not the Ari left behind on Diomedes, but the Ari who found him at his lowest point.

The young girl looked worse for wear. Only twelve years old and marred with all the trauma the Meridian System could muster and curse her with. He knelt in front her. Ari—young, bruised, battered, and all alone—had an inferno in her brown eyes that Kennex knew would only burn brighter as she grew.

"Don't move." Ari pointed at him in command. Bandages covered every inch of her hands and arms. It hid the injuries she sustained from clawing her way out of metal and fire. She turned her back to him and stood tall—fearless.

Kennex shifted so he could continue staring in awe at the only person in his life who made him feel safe. This had been the start. The first moment Kennex felt protected.

"Wanna pick on someone? Huh!? Come on then!" Young Ari snapped at adversaries that couldn't be seen in this ghost of a memory.

After his mother tried to gut him, he was moved into the School to heal. Kennex had only been there a couple days before a collection of older boys decided their new hobby would be bullying him. In this memory, one of them had shoved him to the ground, and Ari swooped in without hesitation.

Ari lunged forward, and her image blurred in broken movements he could only follow due to the memory living in the forefront of his mind. The older boys had blown her off, tried to leave, but even at that age she couldn't let go of a fight. At twelve, Ari only had her anger. With no training, she was a scrawny whirlwind of flailing limbs, teeth, and poorly formed fists. Still, nothing kept her down. Every time she hit the floor, she bounced back up with more fire than she started with. It had left a sick, young Kennex in awe.

The fight ended with the boys running from the feral girl, covered in their fair share of bruises and blood. Ari's blurred image came back into focus as she returned to him. Her face was swelling, nose bleeding but not broken, and her teeth were stained with blood—both hers and theirs.

"If you can't fight, you should get better at running." Ari scoffed. Kennex

laughed at the familiar words. She spat on the floor, and Kennex couldn't stop staring at her small hands. Already soaked in blood. Young Ari limped away.

His mouth opened, and the word from his memory left before he could stop it.

"Stay."

It was the first word Kennex had spoken to Ari, but she never heard it.

- EIGHT -

s dying was becoming a habit, Kennex made the mental note to request the Ascendants allow him to wake up in the same location from now on. He was sick of opening his eyes to a new ceiling. With a grunt, more of annoyance than pain, he sat up in bed. This was not Lyris' bedroom. Not by a longshot.

It was spacious. White walls with plain and boring décor. The bed, larger than any he had ever laid in, was centered in the room. Crisp, clean navy sheets covered him. In the right corner of the room was an arch that led into a bathroom.

"Where the frak am I now?" Kennex muttered as he slid out of bed. Walking to the arch, he found no pain or aches in his bones. Most days he woke up in some form of discomfort. It was jarring enough that Kennex paused in place and stretched his limbs—looking for any soreness. He finished by bending his neck to the left then right, but there wasn't even enough tension for him to pop.

Continuing his path, he confirmed that a bathroom lay beyond the arch, and it was disgustingly overdone. The shower was larger than his living space on Acheron. Granted, after quick use of it, he decided the first thing he would do when he got back to Ari was build one into their stash house. Kennex didn't hesitate to use the amenities the bathroom was stocked with. The owner of this place could surely afford a few missing resources.

As he roughly dried his hair with a towel, he noticed another arch on the other side of the large bathroom—contents hidden in darkness. Kennex padded toward it, still drying his hair, and the light turned on when he stepped through the archway. His eyes widened at the racks of clothes hanging from the wall, but surprise melted into a sneer.

Nobody needs this much of anything in their life.

Lyris' husband's clothes were tossed onto the counter waiting for him, but the clothes here looked closer to his size. Kennex dropped the towel and grabbed something that felt more like him—a plain, dark gray shirt and black pants. He pulled on a pair of boots and bit back a groan of relief. These were worlds above the sneaker styled shoe he had barely squeezed into. He froze, fully dressed. The outfit was like his usual wear, but the high quality was abnormal on his skin. Too heavy, too soft.

Kennex forced his feet to carry him out of the bathroom then out of the bedroom.

The rest of the home matched the room. Grand and imperial. Smooth, white walls decorated with paintings rather than rust or holes. The floor was a light brown wood. Kennex could count on one hand the times he had walked on a wooden floor. The house was broad and open. A kitchen melting into a living room, like Lyris' home, but the similarities ended there.

The kitchen was filled with shiny, silver appliances and dark blue cabinets. It was elevated from the rest of the room. Down four steps into the living room sat navy couches, three of various sizes, on a black carpet with a low table nestled between it all. Kennex spotted the books from the library resting there. The furthest wall was one large window displaying rolling hills of dark green treetops. Kennex drifted toward the glass. Illyarium was well known for its forests. There was no large body of water on this world, but it was said parts of this immense forest were as deep and dark as the oceans on Wricala.

"Took you long enough."

Kennex's head snapped in time to see a woman step out of a door in the kitchen holding a box. Cool, violet eyes glared at him and a flash of them standing over him while dying flooded his mind. Kennex reached for a hand cannon that was not there.

"Relax," she scoffed.

The woman was average in height and fit. An Ascendant. He didn't recognize her, but some part of him knew. Her skin was brown, unmarred and beautiful, and her black hair was long and straight. Her white shirt left her shoulders and midriff exposed. She wore a long, matching skirt with a slit on the left that revealed her leg.

Kennex stomped over to her. "*Relax*? You killed me for no reason."

"I had a reason. You attacked X'ael, so I killed you. We're even now," she replied and pulled out dishes out from the cabinets. With her comfort in the setting, his initial thought was the house being hers, but the closet full of men's clothing made him doubtful. Kennex glanced around again, listening for anyone else, but it seemed they were the only ones in the house.

"Those don't seem equivalent."

"Then kill me, edger." She rolled her eyes. It had been some time since he was mocked with Inner Orbit's nickname for anyone in Outer Orbit. A slow smirk spread across her face. "Or try to, I should say."

"Where is—" A large door, the exit out of this prison on the opposite of the room from the large window, swung open, and the person he planned to ask about breezed in.

Vira nodded. "Oh, good. You're finally up."

A man slipped in from behind her, and Kennex recognized the similar features. He was related to the Ascendant who killed him. He was shorter than Kennex but broader. Like the woman, he had brown skin and black hair. Unlike the woman, his violet eyes were filled with mirth.

"Huh. He's smaller than I pictured." The man chuckled. Kennex furrowed his brow. He and Vira came closer, and the man offered his hand in greeting. "I'm Brin." Kennex eyed the man's tight, gray muscle shirt and matching leggings with black shorts over it. He ignored the welcoming gesture. Brin let out a low whistle and pulled his hand back. "Okay then. You already met my twin—Lee. She's the one who killed you. Sorry about that."

"Don't apologize for things I'm not sorry for," Lee snapped.

Brin held his arms out as he laughed. "If I didn't apologize on your behalf, we'd have more enemies than friends."

The house belonged to the twins. He must have woken in Brin's room. Kennex found his eyes bouncing between the three of them. Making the leap in logic that Brin was an Ascendant like his sister was not difficult. No specific sign gave away an Ascendant, and Kennex hadn't been particularly good at recalling them from news broadcasts. As he stood amidst these three immortals, there was a ringing at the back of his mind. A warning siren plaguing his thoughts.

Vira passed him to the couches. "We don't have much time."

"What do you mean?" Kennex asked without letting his eyes leave the twins. Vira didn't offer an answer. Instead, she marched past him again with the books now in her arms. She settled at the kitchen island where Lee was cutting a purple root.

"You're researching something Otradu related." Vira dropped the books onto the counter.

Kennex flinched at the rough treatment of the aged binding. Lee's eyes were drawn to the noise, and they widened in surprise only to furrow into a glare. She twisted the knife to point at Vira. "Are you out of your damned mind tossing those around?" Vira pressed the pad of her finger to the knife tip and pushed it down. "Where did you even get books that old?"

"Library."

"You aren't allowed—"

"He is." Vira pointed at Kennex who stiffened. "He's a tier one Ascendant."

The shock on Lee's face was transient and shifted to annoyance as she returned to her cutting board—swiping the root slices into a bowl. Brin gave an appreciative nod while sizing him up. Kennex grumbled, "I am not a tier one Ascendant. Hells, I'm not—"

"We don't have the time for your denial right now, new light," Vira sighed. She tapped the top book and bobbed her head to the cooking twin. "Lee speaks Otri."

Kennex barked out a laugh.

"I'm serious."

"There's not a Stellotrian in the system that would spend time teaching a Yarian Otri. Especially not a *fraking* Ascendant."

Lee lifted her violet gaze from the red paste-like sauce she was making and hissed a string of words that Kennex wouldn't have caught even if he had been prepared. It was rare to find a Yarian who could speak a word or two let alone be fluent. For one, Stellotrians were not keen on sharing their culture, and even if they were, the language itself was the most complicated Kennex had witnessed.

"She taught herself." Vira lightly elbowed Lee with a grin of pride. It may have been the first time he saw a smile reach her eyes. Brin wandered over to his sister and leaned over her to grab a root that he dipped into the sauce before crunching in his mouth. "Now, tell Lee what info you need so she can figure it out."

"Why would I tell her?"

"Why would I help him?"

The statements were spoken simultaneously followed by a pause silent enough to hear Brin crunch down on another root.

Vira sighed, "Look, new light, your options aren't great." Kennex locked his jaw and forced his gaze down. "And, Lee, you already killed the poor screwhead. You're even now."

"Being even doesn't mean I want to provide aid," Lee argued.

Kennex preferred to do his own research. He was not a man of faith, but Ari was waiting. Actually, worse, she wouldn't be waiting. Ari wasn't the kind to sit idly by which meant she was traversing the system with no back up and Recluse breathing down her neck. Kennex didn't have the time to follow his preferences.

"The faster I get the answers I need, the sooner I'm off this planet." Kennex forced the plea out. He lifted his gaze to find Lee staring at him skeptically.

She shifted her jaw, left then right, before pushing out an aggravated sigh. Lee grabbed the top book off the pile. "What information do you need?"

"Anything about *see-ames*, including a translation of the word."

Lee cracked the book open but paused with a tilt of her head. "*See-ames*?"

Kennex was confident he had pronounced it as the Curator did. He nodded. "Hmm." Lee buried herself back into the book.

"Good." Vira clapped her hands. "Now, while she reads, we need to talk, new light."

"Again with that *fraking* nickname."

"Brin and Lee are a part of my fireteam," Vira continued as if he hadn't spoken. "Malachi putting you under my care is the equivalent of him putting you on this team." Kennex opened his mouth, and she cut him off. "Aether, I fraking know. You don't want to be an Ascendant and you don't want to be on a fireteam."

Kennex shook his head. "No—I mean, yes, that's true, but...You call the Curator by his first name? Isn't that frowned upon?"

It wasn't Illyarium law that the Curator be referenced by his title, but it was a measure of respect or habit. Kennex expected Ascendants to be annoying with their degree of devotion and it confused him that it didn't seem to be the case.

"Yeah," Brin answered with a mouthful of food. Bits sprayed out in Lee's direction, and she shoved him away without breaking focus.

"He's not a fan of being referred to by his actual name," Vira added.

"Then why do it?"

Brin swallowed, then answered, "Spite, mostly."

"Ascendants, golden soldiers of Aether's Light, are spiteful to the Curator? Isn't he your boss?" Kennex scoffed. The serious, though mocking, question was followed by laughter. Brin was the loudest and even Lee cracked a small smile without looking up.

Vira chuckled, "Are you unwaveringly loyal to your boss?" Kennex gave her that. If he equated Ascendants to the Curator as Lucky Fox and Venom were to Recluse, the laughter made sense. Eighty percent of the decisions Ari made in life were to spite the Dracck. "You have a lot to learn."

"So, I'm gathering," Kennex muttered. He pulled out one of the stools tucked under the kitchen island to sit on. Vira copied the casual pose by leaning her hip against the counter, ankles and arms crossed.

"The Curator is not the man you think he is."

"He's not an egotistical, power-hungry bastard with a superiority complex?"

Brin waved a finger at him. "Yeah, no, he is those things."

"Malachi is an *Ascendant*," Vira said. "Only tier one and tier two Ascendants know this."

Kennex didn't believe it. Not the bit about the Curator hiding his immortality. He always knew Aether's Light was darker than they portrayed themselves, and he didn't struggle with swallowing the news that the leader of said corrupt organization was a liar. Kennex's doubt laid in the insinuation that a secret this large could be successfully kept.

"How long—"

"He's at least two thousand years old. I'd guess more," Brin cut in.

Kennex laughed dryly at the prospect, "Please. The Curator has been the same person since the dawn of Aether's Light, and *nobody* but two tiers of Ascendants know? Yeah, right."

"No Ascendant under his wing would ever betray his secret," Vira replied. Kennex rolled his eyes, and she reached out to tap the counter and command his attention back. "It isn't respect. At least, not in all cases. Some, yes, but for most it's self-preservation. Even if he wasn't immortal, he's the fraking Curator. He has loyal followers all throughout Inner, Middle, and even Outer Orbit." Kennex stiffened at the reminder. "Not to mention his seat on the Illyarium High Council. Malachi has the system in his hands, and you don't double cross a man with that kind of power."

He saw the logic. Besides, it was hypocritical of him to judge an Ascendant for falling into line when he had done the same with Recluse for the last decade.

Vira pulled her hand back and shook her head. "You keep your mouth shut about it, new light, and you might survive to see your friend."

"What could he possibly do to me?" Kennex retaliated. "I can't die anymore." A tense silence that ensued, leaving him baffled.

Ascendants could not bleed, they could not die, and he assumed this left them fearless. Egotistical maniacs, sure, but fearless ones. The picture they painted in this kitchen was different from the one in his mind.

"Whatever. I don't care." Kennex snorted. "Not about that, not about him being an Ascendant, not about—" Mentions of the scene on Diomedes were about to leave his lips, but he swallowed them. "*I don't care.*" He waved his hand once, brushing the topic away, and moved on. "Now, what else? What else do I need to know to survive here in the court until I get my answers and can leave?"

Lee scoffed and set the journal down. "It's means 'gods.' Bye."

"Wait, what?"

"*See-ames* translates to 'gods' as far as I can guess. It references Aether," she repeated herself. "Good-bye, and good riddance."

Kennex considered this information. He supposed he should have assumed the Curator, religious icon of the Meridian System, would give him some call back to Aether. He grumbled under his breath as Lee was scolded by Vira.

"I'm sorry, V, why are we protecting the edger again?"

"I told you. He's part of—"

"Our fireteam?" Lee pointed at him accusingly. "He clearly doesn't think so, so why should I?" She slammed a hand on the counter. "I get that we're desperate for a fourth, but we can't possibly be *this* desperate."

Vira sighed, "Lee, this is about more than just completing the team."

Kennex didn't appreciate being spoken about as if he weren't sitting right in front of them. He leaned forward, arm on the counter, and snatched their attention with a scoff. He focused his glare primarily on Lee. "I didn't ask for any of this, I don't fraking want it. If you have such a problem with me, then give me my books and I'll leave. I never asked to be brought to your house in the first place."

Lee gave him a deadpanned look and crossed her arms. "This is *your* dorm, you fraking screwhead."

The news caught him off guard and he glanced to Vira who nodded in confirmation. Kennex looked around his lavish surroundings and tried to fathom the idea of this being his.

"You're clueless, and then you take an attitude whenever we try to help."

Kennex snapped back into the moment. His head spun to find her, and he guffawed, "Are you kidding me? *My* attitude?" This time he pointed at her. "You're the one picking fights. How was I supposed to know this is mine? Especially with you moving around in the kitchen like you owned the place!"

"I'm sorry." Her tone did not sound apologetic. "Was I supposed to just sit on the couch hungry and bored as you slept the day away?"

"I was only sleeping because you *fraking killed me*!"

The shrill beeping of Vira's vambrace interrupted the fight. Brin blew out a loud breath of air and threw his hands up. "Oh, thank Aether. Perfect timing."

"We have to leave, or we'll be late. Can you two put a pin in this for now?" Vira took a moment to glare at Lee and Kennex individually. They both gave curt nods, and she walked away muttering. "Arguing like fraking children."

Lee left, but Kennex hesitated. He stared at the books on the counter, weighing his options, and a sharp whistle made him glance up. Vira called for him to leave the books behind. As Kennex rose from the stool, he decided to ignore her. Peeling away to the room he woke in, he stole a cross-body bag from the closet. After stuffing the books into it, Kennex agreed to leave with hopes to never see this suffocating dorm again.

- NINE -

Vira, Brin, and Lee waited for him outside the door. There were five other dorms off this hall, all spaced enormously apart, and the group moved as a pack to the floor's lift. Like the one leading up to the Curator's grand office, it was made of glass. Kennex rested his hands on the rails to study the view—he could see the entirety of the Court of Aether and beyond.

The dorm building was nestled at the top of a large hill. A courtyard sat directly below them, and it connected to another via a set of stairs. It was as if this entire hill had various ledges cascading down like a waterfall until it reached a golden gate at the bottom. This island of land was a sharp contrast to the marble and glass it sat beside. If it weren't for the tall stone fence encircling the area, separating it from Sector One, he would have assumed this area was external to the court. The buildings he recognized were the obscenely tall tower, the Hall of Murals, of which only a portion could be seen, and the entrance for the Adherent Village.

"We're in Haven," Vira explained. She motioned through the glass as it descended. She pointed out smaller landmarks below as he tried to make out the details of Sector One beyond the wall. The portion of the city closest to the court was rather drab and plain with buildings that had no definitive detail. Further out from the court, the buildings grew taller, larger, but remained rather plain. He could see the spoke of the Overflow Ring in the distance, the only structure taller than the Curator's tower, stretching all the way up to its connection on the ring.

The lift reached a level that kept him from spotting anything new, and when it hit the bottom floor, he asked, "Haven?"

Lee snorted and stepped out first. "He wasn't even listening to you, V."

Kennex glared at the back of her head, but Vira nudged him to follow. "It's fine. Haven is where we live. It's technically in the Court of Aether, but it's a separate marked off area. Only Ascendants are allowed in. The exception being a few adherents and acolytes who work here."

Kennex glanced back at the dorm building to admire its full height. Vira, Brin, and Lee didn't wait for him, and he jogged after to keep up with their quick pace. They veered left in the courtyard, and he took notice of the living and rather simple flowers and trees. The greenery was beautiful, but Kennex found it surprisingly plain for what he expected the Ascendants to reside among.

"This is the back way out of Haven." Vira motioned to where the path came to an end at another lift they entered without pause. "It's the quickest way to get us to where we're going."

"And where exactly is that?"

"The Cathedral."

Kennex resisted the urge to audibly groan. The doors of the lift slid open for them to exit, and the difference between the top of the lift to the bottom was stark and disorienting. They walked across the polished, white stone path into the monotone fake gardens.

Nobody had to explain the Cathedral to him. Even if the name wasn't self-explanatory, Kennex recognized it as the most infamous place of worship in the system for any follower of Aether's Light. All the Curator's broadcasted sermons came from there. Kennex didn't appreciate what could be so special about a building, but there were followers that crossed the system to visit.

The Cathedral was audacious and absorbent as he expected it to be. This was by far the most elaborate building in the Court of Aether. Bricks of white and tan mixed with marble slabs to form elaborate shapes. The main entrance from the court at the top of a short half flight of stairs was an open arch at least six stories tall. The feature that stood out the most to him was the color. Whereas the rest of the court stayed in the monochromatic theme of white, gold, or black, the Cathedral had splashes of vibrant color. The roofing was a rich purple jutting up in sharp triangles and the numerous, large windows were made of intricate stained glass.

"Come on. We're late," Vira chided as he lagged.

"You keep saying that, but you won't tell me what we're late for," Kennex countered with slowed steps. Vira paused. Brin and Lee waited a step ahead of her.

"Sermon," Lee chimed. "We're late for Sermon."

Kennex stopped at the answer, but Vira grasped him by the elbow and dragged him along. He realized the others walking into the Cathedral with them were also Ascendants. The ringing at the back of his head was more pronounced. Vira jostled his bag and he pulled himself out of her hold.

"I told you to leave the books at home," Vira sighed.

Kennex had no plans of returning to that dorm, and he had no plans of returning these books back to the library.

Inside matched the exterior in grandeur. High ceilings with stained glass windows allowed rays of Sol, all in shades of soft color, to glitter in the air above them. The navy tiled floors had a shine, and the walls were covered in physical paintings housed in aged, golden frames. Kennex's steps slowed to study one, but Vira tugged him along again.

"I don't want to go to sermon," Kennex whined.

"This isn't a usual sermon. It's *Sermon*." Brin emphasized the word as if that would clarify the meaning. "It's held weekly for Ascendants."

Vira bumped her shoulder into his making his frown deepen. "Stop pouting, new light. It doesn't last long."

Kennex bit his tongue and continued to follow them. Vira and Brin acted as if they were all old friends. He hadn't decided if it baffled or annoyed him. Their presence would be easier to digest if they treated him with the same disdain Lee did.

They passed through another set of grand doors, and it led into a large auditorium that reminded him of the stairs and door into the Curator's balcony. The coliseum styled room with stone benches had a matching stage far below. A spotlight shone down, but Kennex couldn't find the source as the upper ceiling of the room was shrouded in darkness. Hundreds of Ascendants were present, but the room felt barren.

"How many Ascendants stay in the court?" Kennex asked as they descended the stairs.

"Depends. Usually around 500 at any given time." Brin shrugged. He walked beside Kennex as Vira and Lee led them down. "The rest are out and about. Monitoring the system, taking missions, patrolling. The work cycles depend on the assignment given."

"You're given assignments?"

"Yeah," Brin snorted. "You think we were just running around doing whatever we wanted?" Kennex gave a non-committal shrug. It seemed that way. "I wish. But, no, we get assignments, and our team hasn't been shipped off world in ages."

"Why not?"

"We all got promoted a while back. Moved up from tier three to two. So, now we have to fill a full team of four before we're allowed to go on missions." Kennex understood Lee's earlier complaint about a fourth member, and Brin continued on without prompt. "The lowest tier stays here and works guard shifts both in and out of the court. The next tier up usually works in pairs, and they get shipped out to Outer and Middle Orbit for patrol. Our tier works specific missions, and the teams must be a set of at least four."

Kennex nodded. "Tier two. With the navy cloaks?"

"All of us, but you, new light." Brin clapped him on the shoulder with a grin. Kennex shrugged him off and the violet-eyed man just laughed. "I'll grow on you. Maybe not this century, but eventually."

Brin passed him to slide into the row Vira and Lee had chosen, but Kennex stayed planted. His spine stiffened, tension locking him in place, and a gut-wrenching realization pressed down on him. *"Not this century, but maybe next."* The full impact of being Ascendant hit him. Kennex had been so focused on the resurrections that he hadn't processed the other side of it. He couldn't die. He would live forever. Immortal. Even once he left the Court of Aether, found Ari, it was now inevitable that he would one day be without her.

A sharp whistle grabbed his attention. Kennex sucked in a sharp breath and found Vira waving him over. He awkwardly slid down the row into the seat by Brin.

The lighting began to dim as the spotlight grew brighter. Applause ripped through the calm of the room as a slot on the stage opened. The crown on Malachi's helmet came into view. He rose up from the floor as a mist settled around his ankles. Kennex glanced around skeptically, not fully believing the pomp and vanity he was witnessing, but found many of the Ascendants zoned in. Their excitement palpable. Vira, Lee, and Brin clapped passively as he sat motionless.

Malachi lifted his hands and the room stilled.

"My children," Malachi began. "Blessings to you."

"And blessings to Aether," the room chanted in reply. Kennex couldn't bite back his laugh of disbelief. Ari would have a field day with the knowledge of this practice.

"I know this week has been filled with curiosity and worry." Malachi's voice reverberated through the air in a way that made the words sound like they were being whispered into his ear. Kennex's skin prickled. "Today, I will forgo our usual schedule to address the question in all your minds." He clenched his teeth at the direction this was moving. "You have a new brother. Unexpected, but not unwelcome. Ascendant Kennex Hall, will you join me?"

Eyes found him as whispers rumbled around the room. Brin lightly elbowed him, and Kennex forced himself to stand. Vira hissed at him and yanked his bag off to hold herself. He allowed the motion, wanting to be free of weight, in the case of a fight. Kennex drifted down the stone steps into the sea of curious murmuring.

The estimated 500 Ascendants watched him, and his heart kicked violently against his ribcage. Kennex's fists clenched and unclenched as he craved the comfort of his suit and helmet. In this state, immortal or not, he was vulnerable.

Malachi's arms opened wide the second Kennex stepped onto the stage. He stopped midway, but the leader did not allow him the comfort of distance. Malachi drifted closer until a hand clasped onto the back of Kennex's neck. Firm but not painful. Almost an act of reassurance. His hand twitched as he held back his instinct to shove the Curator off. Kennex was outnumbered, and he was not a fool.

"Kennex comes from the Port of Acheron," Malachi announced. Mumbles of shock followed. "Yes. The furthest point of Outer Orbit—one step from Wild Space. Like many of those on the edges of our system, he is understandably wary of us. People fear what they do not know."

"It's not fear," Kennex mumbled.

Hatred and fear were not comparable in this scenario.

Malachi hummed, leaving a silence that Kennex could fill, but Kennex bit his tongue.

The moment passed and Malachi continued, "Our influence, our protection, does not fully reach that far into Outer Orbit. We are stretched too thin, and souls we swore to save suffer for our lack of reach. But," Malachi raised a finger, "perhaps that is why Aether has made this mysterious decision."

The attention the Curator held was difficult to fathom but hearing him speak Kennex began to understand. Hate aside, he could not deny the strength underlying the soft words hanging in the air. Malachi's voice was like a song the crowd could not pull themselves away from.

"I believe that is why young Kennex Hall ascended." Malachi lightly squeezed the back of his neck as his other hand settled over Kennex's chest—over the golden scars hidden by his shirt. "Aether is bringing us an opportunity to be better. Bringing us a connection to the worlds that hide from our light! Why else would your newest brother be discovered in the dark? If not to be the bearer of salvation to those who remain blinded?"

A thunderous roar of applause met the hypothetical question. Kennex locked his jaw and tried to turn his head to scan the room of dimly lit faces, but Malachi's hand tightened again. It kept him staring straight ahead.

Softly, Malachi whispered to him, "Do not spare your gaze to those beneath you, Kennex."

Malachi sidestepped, back to the center of the stage, dragging Kennex along. When they settled, the Curator spoke again. "Ascendant Herring will walk you through the final necessary announcements. But, take this with you my children... A new era is upon us, and Aether's love will touch every corner of this system."

Kennex flinched at a hiss of machinery. His last sight was an unfamiliar Ascendant with a black cloak stepping onto the stage as he sunk beneath the ground in Malachi Moretti's grasp.

- TEN -

"I have no interest in being your savior," Kennex spat.

When they reached solid flooring, he untangled himself from Malachi's hold. They were below ground based on the rough, stone walls. The room was circular, like the one above, but significantly smaller. Torches filled the space with a warm light and a stone table jutted out from the wall. It was covered in jars, books, and plants.

"Why not?" Malachi shrugged. Kennex scoffed as Malachi approached the table. "Kennex, you are filled with *light*. You no longer need to exist in the shadows. You can rise and be who you were fated to be."

"I like who I am. I have no interest in changing."

"Did you find your answers?"

"I hardly had the time."

Malachi chuckled. "Right. Of course. You went through another resurrection." He opened a jar filled with yellow powder. "Ascendant Brylee Crézen has always had trouble with her temper." He poured the dust onto the table and shaped the small pile into a flattened circle. Kennex stepped closer to watch. "You have some information though."

"Gods," Kennex offered Lee's half-assed translation. "*See-ames* seems to refer to Aether."

"Correct." Malachi chuckled at a joke Kennex wasn't privy to. "Though there are some who would argue the verbiage." He used the tip of the taloned ring on his thumb to draw shapes in the powder. "Kennex, I only spoke truth when I announced to your brethren that you were taken from the dark, and you have come into more than just immortality." Malachi glanced over his shoulder. "You have come into *power*."

Steeling his nerve, Kennex nodded. "And what power is that, *Ascendant Malachi*?" The Curator's hand paused in its motions. "That's right. I know." He scoffed. "Self-righteous bastard. You think you're above it all? What gives you the right—"

Knocking interrupted him.

The heavy door groaned and X'ael entered. Just the sight of the immortal made Kennex's entire body tense. He grasped the charm around his neck.

X'ael paid him no mind. In fact, the Ascendant rushed past him to kneel before the Curator. "Sir, I apologize. It was not my intent to fail you. I—"

Malachi held out the hand not drawing in powder, and X'ael went silent. From where he stood, Kennex saw the tremor in the bowing immortal's frame. This wasn't the first punishment he had been forced to witness. Though similar in tension, there was one clear distinction. When Ari was forced to her knees, forced to listen to Recluse's sharp tongue, she never trembled or bowed her head—she did not allow Recluse that power. Kennex sneered at X'ael's weakness.

"I asked you to bring me the child." Malachi did not yell. His voice was calm and steady. "But when Kennex Hall ascended you chose to bring me only him."

"The ascension was so unusual. I assumed you would want—"

"I told you what I wanted, X'ael."

"I apologize, sir."

"Not only did you leave the child behind, but you also attempted to kill Ari Barlow."

"I—I panicked, sir. I wanted to bring you the newly ascended and I did not think—"

"X'ael," Malachi lifted his hand from the powder, "I do not need you to think." He grasped the immortal by his jaw and lifted his gaze up. X'ael's abnormal red eyes widened. "I need you to *listen*."

Kennex waited for pain. He was eager for it. He wanted to watch X'ael suffer. However, Malachi didn't attack. His sharp ring drew a triangle between X'ael's eyes, but the glowing injury didn't even cause the Ascendant to flinch. The hold on the immortal's jaw was loose and supportive.

"You failed me, X'ael."

"I'm sorry," X'ael gasped. "Mercy."

"I am not angry, my child, only disappointed."

X'ael looked as if had been struck. Agony flooded his features. Malachi pulled his hand away and X'ael collapsed to his hands as he cried apologies. Kennex scoffed at the whimpering immortal. The small sliver of respect he held for him, the kind held for an adversary, vanished.

"Leave us," Malachi said. Kennex initially assumed the instruction was meant for him, but X'ael struggled to his feet before shuffling out. Kennex didn't realize he was watching X'ael's escape until Malachi called for him.

"You are unimpressed."

"He's pathetic," Kennex snapped.

"Seeking the approval of a father is pathetic?" Malachi asked. "Of course. You and Ari never bowed to Recluse. Neither of you ever whimpered or begged for his mercy."

"No, we didn't," Kennex replied. He shook his head. "And Recluse was *not* our father."

"He was the closest thing either of you had at that time, was he not?"

"A father doesn't do what he did to us."

"He made you watch." Malachi fully turned around to face him. "He'd make you watch as he buried his talons into Ari's tender flesh—"

"Shut up," Kennex growled.

"Leave you helpless as she bled on his desk in the aftermath of Ari's breaking." Malachi spoke quicker, not allowing him the breath to cut in. "Or he'd beat you as a means to an end. Never a direct punishment to you. *No.* You were just the pawn he used to get Ari to obey, am I right? Even in the punishments you faced, you were a *passive* being. Never the focus, never a person in your own accord, but simply a device to further Ari's fall."

"*I said, shut up!*"

The silence that followed was painful. Kennex had a ringing in his ears as if a bomb had gone off. The pounding of his heart stole his breath with every painful beat.

Malachi crossed his arms. "I am sorry, Kennex. My intention was not to hurt you. Just to voice the truth." He tilted his head. "Perhaps, I should let you return to your fireteam." Kennex didn't have the peace of mind to argue the title. His teeth were still grinding together. "I, unfortunately, cannot allow you to leave here on your own accord. Not yet. But I will leave you with another word to further your studies."

Kennex didn't understand, but he wasn't left with time to ponder. Malachi waved his hand, and the flames in the room extinguished—leaving him in pitch-black. Kennex took a step back as his eyes failed to adjust. Dimly, pinpoints of light appeared above him. Stars. They glittered as faint lines reached from one to another. His eyes focused on one directly above him. Four points connected like an elongated diamond. It was the last constellation he could fathom before a hand wrapped around his throat and a hot breath fanned down his neck.

"*Eunim.*"

A crack of bone, and he was gone.

- ELEVEN -

Kennex startled awake. His chest heaved for air that did not bring him relief. He was seated in a familiar chair in Recluse's office. Confusion snapped into panic as a sharp scream shattered the calm reality he tried to cling to. Recluse manhandled Ari across the room toward his desk. She thrashed in his hold—kicking and screaming.

"Ari!" He attempted to jump up only to find he was pinned to his seat by hands on his arms and shoulders. "No!"

"Get the frak off of me!" Ari screamed.

Recluse roared rather than spoke and slammed Ari face down onto his desk. With ease from practice, he ripped the back of her shirt open. Kennex screamed again as Ari stiffened and froze in place. Her warm brown eyes, flooded with fear, met his. He couldn't reassure her. They learned early that Recluse would worsen the punishment if he tried. So instead, Kennex let his gaze echo every word he'd whisper to her after.

It's okay.

You're gonna be okay.

You're not alone.

I'm here.

I'm here.

I'm here.

Ari's teeth clenched as a talon buried into her skin. She did not scream. She did not beg. She did not whimper. Where the punishment would usually end, Recluse continued. Kennex gaped in raw shock as the vision of Recluse shimmered into something wrong. Too many claws raked into Ari's back, wild blue eyes drained into the same shade of red as Ari's blood, too many golden fangs elongated over curled lips. Black ichor dripped from his maw, and she screamed—a sound that tore his own chest to ribbons—as Recluse began to eat her alive.

"Kennex!"

"No, no, no." Kennex was desperate as he tried to reach her. The hands pinning him pushed down harder each time he thrashed. "Stop!" This wasn't happening. This didn't happen. The rage that filled him was not hot and burning. It was cold, sharp, and concrete. *"Stop!"*

A wave of white light burst from where he sat.

Kennex fell forward on his hands and knees, gasping for air, as silence enveloped him. The black stone under him was recognizable, and he found himself happy to be in Joon.

"I did not create that nightmare. You did."

Kennex's head snapped up as Recluse walked around him.

"You," he hissed between clenched teeth. With a cry, he pushed up to tackle his old employer. Kennex fell through the figure of Recluse who disappeared in a mist and landed with a grunt. A few feet away, Recluse formed again.

"Is this why you had me take this form? To attack?" Recluse's voice tutted. "Sad."

Kennex studied the Dracck. The boxy patterns on his loud, red suit were moving, and he was larger than Kennex knew him to be. The mimic had created him too tall, too broad.

"I don't want this," Kennex gasped, haggard. Ari's screams still looping in his mind. "This isn't what I asked for."

"One does not ask for their destiny to find them."

"Gotta be fraking kidding me," Kennex mumbled under his breath as he struggled to rise. Unsteady on his feet, he shook his head. "Get the hells out of my head." The mimic chuckled. "You weren't here last time. I don't want you here ever again."

"I come when you call."

Kennex opened his mouth to yell but paused. Arguing with the mimic, whether it be a creature caught in his head or a concept of his own creation, seemed pointless. Exhausted, he waved his hand. "Out. I want out. Let me wake up."

"I am not keeping you here." The mimic shrugged. Recluse's towering figure drew closer and Kennex forced himself not to step back. When it settled beside him, the mimic hummed. "You enjoyed having a memory of Ari. It brought you comfort, yes?"

"Don't—"

His voice fell on deaf ears, and Ari appeared. Memory or not, she became his sole focus. She was older than last time, and the fresh scar on her face gave him a good guess of the timeframe. Sixteen. He hadn't been there when Recluse slammed her head into the desk, only witnessed the results. The injury was healing well, irritation and bruising remained, which meant she was close to turning seventeen. This was right before they were promoted to task runners.

"Again," the mimic spoke as Recluse.

Ari grinned as her ghost reached down to pull a blurry figure up by the front of their shirt. Kennex couldn't remember who the person was or what they had done to Recluse to warrant this. Through this entire moment, Kennex had only been looking to Ari. She pummeled her fist into the person begging for mercy at Recluse's order.

"Why are you showing me this memory?" Kennex demanded.

"Why not?" the mimic responded with a shrug. "Does it bother you?"

Ari's onslaught never paused, never broke, until Recluse commanded it. With one final punch, blood splattered up onto her features. She used her arm to swipe it away, but her smile remained. Her hands, wrapped tightly by him moments prior, were stained red. Kennex hated this memory— hated the thought that was tied to it.

Why is she enjoying this?

Kennex stared at Ari who only looked to Recluse. This was the first time Kennex felt fear that he would lose his partner. Not to distance or death, but to the brutality. It was when he truly realized they needed to leave. He spent the next seven years finding seconds to plead this point with her only for it to be cast aside.

Kennex should've tried harder.

"She's doing what she has to," Kennex said firmly.

"Yes. You did as well." The mimic chuckled. "But you never took pleasure in it as she did."

Ari's eyes drifted to him, and he recognized the brief flicker of shame.

"Ari is a good person."

"Sometimes." The mimic brushed its hand through the air and Ari's features faded. "Sometimes not." It turned to face him. "You were the nagging conscious tethered to her. Now, without you, she is free to follow her instinct. That's what you fear, is it not, Kennex? That without you guiding her, she is running reckless about the system seeking trouble wherever she goes and leaving a trail of blood and bodies behind her."

Kennex shook his head. "Stop talking about her like you know her."

"I do know her," the mimic said. A shadow formed as Recluse's figure grew larger. It eclipsed him. "Through your memories, I *know* Ari Barlow." Kennex stumbled back a step as he strained to meet the mimic's gaze. "The source of my information is *your* mind, Kennex. I only speak, what you have once thought."

An argument died on his lips as Recluse's taloned hand slammed down on top of him and crushed him through the stone floor and into nothing.

- TWELVE -

He returned to the same bed, but this time he did not linger.

Kennex rolled to his feet and marched to the door. Stepping out into the main space, he paused. Lee sat on the couch reading the journal from Otradu, Vira was on the couch opposite of her watching the news on a holoscreen, and Brin stood at the counter eating.

"Oh, look. He's up." Brin pointed a fork at him. "You know, if you let us kill you about nine or ten more times, your resurrections will be instantaneous."

"Why are you here?" Kennex demanded.

"You have the largest dorm," Vira answered. "Besides, as part of my fireteam—"

"I'm not. I'm not on your team, and I'm not an Ascendant. I'm leaving."

Vira called after him, but it was Brin who settled a hand on his shoulder with a word of appeasement. Kennex spun on his heel and punched him. Brin hissed as golden light shimmered from the break of skin at the bridge of his nose.

He hated close quarters combat. As soon as he laid claim on a hand cannon, he avoided it altogether. It seemed an unnecessary risk. Kennex was beginning to understand the addiction though. Punching the Ascendant lessened the pain rattling in his chest.

With a snarl, Brin lunged forward and tackled Kennex. The immortal was quick despite his size. Kennex took two blows to the face before he was able to throw his arms up to block. In the brief window when Brin pulled his arm back to gain power, Kennex shoved him to the side so they rolled. He palmed Brin's face to slam back. A loud crack echoed as his skull bounced off the floor.

With his opponent in a daze, Kennex cocked back to punch again but a cold chain wrapped around his neck. He grasped at the metal, choking, as he was yanked back. Lee stared down at him, chain skillfully wrapped around her arm, and Kennex flinched when she lifted her leg. Rather than kill him, she set the flat portion of her heeled foot against his forehead.

"Please don't kill my brother," She tsked. "He gets pissy about it."

"Vira, let me go!" Brin roared from across the room. "Get off me!"

The immortal continued to holler, but it grew more faint until it disappeared followed by a click of the door. Lee removed her foot and when she dropped her arms the chain around his neck loosened. Kennex gasped for breath and sat up while trying to detangle himself from the metal.

"Where did they go?" Kennex asked, voice hoarse.

"Somewhere to calm down." Lee walked back over to the couch and sat down. "Probably Rakerby's." The answer wasn't helpful. Kennex drifted to crash on the couch across from Lee. "Stop rubbing your throat. It's pathetic. You're fine."

Kennex hadn't realized he was still cradling his neck. His hand fell as the pain rapidly ebbed away. He cleared his throat and noted her chain wasn't on the couch with her. "Where is—"

Without looking up from the book, she held her hand out and the chain materialized, landing ready in her waiting grasp.

Kennex's eyes widened in recognition. "X'ael—"

"It's compartmentalization of matter." Lee tossed the chain up and it vanished again.

"Like magik?"

Lee glanced up to ensure he saw her mocking glare. "No, edger. Like *science*." She twisted her arm to reveal the faint glowing lights of a dermal implant. "My father invented them some time ago. It's rarely used."

"Why?" Kennex couldn't imagine why anyone would turn down an implant if it could allow the disintegration and reintegration of matter itself.

"Because it's difficult to master, and if you frak it up you compartmentalize yourself into a void of space and time." Lee smiled in the least friendly fashion. "Only a handful of people, like my brother and myself, have mastered it on their own."

"People like X'ael."

"No. He never puzzled it out himself," Lee replied. "I taught him."

Kennex leaned forward, elbows on his knees. "What is with you and X'ael? You can't possibly like him. Even Vira called him a sniveling weasel."

"Don't talk about him like that!" Lee snapped. Regret flashed in her eyes the second the words left her. She buried herself back into the journal. "You just don't... You wouldn't get it." Kennex didn't find any empathy for the Ascendant. Lee shut the journal and looked back up, regret shifting to resolve. "He wasn't always like this. Okay? He was—It's fraking Malachi who is the problem. *Not* X'ael."

"They can both be problems."

Lee shook her head. "Well, X'ael wasn't. Not until after we ascended, and Derrik Russell left."

"Left? Didn't he retire?" Kennex snorted.

"Malachi strong armed him into retiring, but Derrik ran after the public ceremony." Lee shrugged. "He's existing out in Wild Space right now or something. I only know that because Vira told me, and it isn't information we should have. Don't pass it along."

Kennex was too busy picturing the once Golden Boy of the Meridian System toughing it in Outer Orbit to take Lee's warning seriously. On Ari's behalf, Kennex hoped Ascendant Russell was fraking miserable in whatever hole he crawled into.

"Anyways, Ascendant Russell was Malachi's right-hand man, so when he left, there was a hole to fill."

Kennex shook his head. "If you're trying to convince me that X'ael was normal at some point in life, or make me pity him, it's not going to work."

"I don't need you to..." Lee's voice trailed off. A grimace Kennex labeled as embarrassment flittered across her features, but it was gone too quick.

"Defending him is a habit of mine. I know he killed you. I know he killed your friend—"

"Ari is alive. He didn't kill her."

"He tried, and I'm sorry," Lee blurted. Though the words were pushed through her teeth as if it pained her, Kennex caught the sincerity.

He shook his head. "Why isn't that a habit you can break? Friend or not, you know he isn't good. Hells, he isn't right in the head."

"X'ael was my partner," Lee said. Kennex heard the quiet click of her teeth clenching as she locked her jaw.

The weight that came with the word "partner" was not lost on him. Ari flashed in his mind, but it was an impulsive thought. Kennex brushed it away. "Were the two of you involved?"

Lee tilted her head mockingly. "Were the two of you?"

It was hardly the first time someone had asked about the parameters of his relationship with Ari. It was, however, the first time he found himself speechless. Lee raised an eyebrow at his silence. An acknowledgement of the question they both dodged.

Kennex dropped his head and sighed. "I need to get out of here."

"That isn't going to happen. Vira won't let you go."

"Why?" His head snapped back up, anger replacing admonishment. "She doesn't seem to care much for Malachi, so why keep me like he asked?"

"Because Vira is too good of a person, and she has a bad habit of adopting sob stories." Lee huffed and used the book in her hand to motion to him. "I know you screwheads from Outer Orbit are obtuse and uneducated, but have you really not figured this out?" Irritation at her backhanded comment on Outer Orbit crawled up his spine, but he locked his jaw to keep his thoughts from spilling out. "Malachi is *never* going to let you leave."

"He said—"

"And you believed him?" Lee let out a harsh laugh. Kennex squirmed. Lee carefully set the journal down on the table and leaned forward to match his pose. Her slender fingers laced together. "Malachi is not to be trusted. He's a snake." She raised a dark eyebrow at him. "You know about snakes, don't you, *Venom*?" Being referred to as his moniker oddly threw him. "He'll strike when your guard is down."

"What can him or any of you possibly do to me? I'm immortal now," Kennex mumbled.

"Immortal, but not untouchable," Lee countered. Kennex furrowed his brow. "Malachi could drop you in a hole and leave you there for a few centuries. Imagine that. Rotting. Starving to death. Dying of thirst. Then you revive, and it starts again. The entire time, every mortal you know is being taken by time. Can you picture it, edger?"

Kennex didn't want to. Even now, with the few options he had, he felt useless to Ari. Being trapped in an enclosed space knowing time was ticking away, leaving him behind, was agony.

"So, when Vira tries to keep you from running off like a fool, it's because she doesn't want to spend her next century with the knowledge that you are buried in the dark." Hands still laced together, she winked and pointed at him. "Though, perhaps the dark is exactly what you like considering your origin."

His first instinct was to argue. The denial was half hanging off his tongue when he swallowed it down. Kennex had a suspicion that Lee would browbeat him.

The dorm's door opened, and Vira sauntered in with a sigh. She clapped her hands then rubbed them together. "So, Brin is cooling off." Vira paused at the top of the few steps leading down to the couches. "That's one crisis nullified. For now." Her head rolled to the side, and she shot him a dry look. "Back to the other."

Kennex dragged a hand down his face. He could still leave. If he managed to slip by the Curator's defenses, out of the Court, then he could be on his merry way. Of course, Malachi would send Ascendants after him. That took him down two paths. Either they catch him, and he ends up in a hole, forgotten by time, or he escapes with them following him. If Ari was traveling with the child like Malachi said, the child he wanted so desperately for some reason, then Kennex could be leading Ascendants right to them.

Regardless of the plan, Kennex would be in the dark, and Lee was wrong when she assumed it was a state he enjoyed. He needed to know. He was *desperate* to know. He hated trying to plan without all the facts.

"Kennex."

Hearing his name spoken with concern made him turn toward Vira. Her arms were crossed, and her eyebrows arched in question. Worry. Kennex struggled to grasp why she'd wear such a look for him, but he didn't mind it.

"My partner and I went to Diomedes to find a distress signal," Kennex began.

Telling the story, having it exist in more minds than just his own, made it real. Since his death on Diomedes, this was the first he had thought through what had happened step by painful step. To Lee and Vira's credit, they did not interrupt. Not when he talked about the dead acolytes, not when he mentioned the girl in the tree with her pet spark, not even when the infusion mauled Ari. They stayed silent and Kennex kept his eyes to the floor to avoid reading their reactions. When he reached the end—*his* end—he finally looked up.

Vira and Lee were not looking at him. They stared at one another in a silent conversation. Kennex cleared his throat and Lee was the first to look his way. Her violet eyes held a softness that hadn't been there before.

"I'm not even going to touch the infusion topic." Lee snorted.

"A problem for another day." Vira replied but her gaze was far away. "We have more pressing matters. Namely, that child."

"Unfortunately, sacrificing a child sounds exactly like Malachi's kind of crazy."

"We need to find out why," Vira added. She sat down on the couch, a cushion away from him, and nodded. "Malachi is a dangerous man, and I am certain he had a reason. Whatever that reason is, crazy or not, doesn't bode well for us."

Kennex's posture straightened. "The clues he's given me hint at it. Ari is in danger, according to him, and it all has to do with the kid." He rubbed the back of his head, his next words spoken mostly to himself. "I knew we should've just left. We never should've searched for the damn kid."

"Well, we'll find the answers," Lee announced. She gave Vira a nod then looked back to him. "I'm in. Officially."

"Really?" Kennex asked. He almost questioned it, but the answer came to him before he could. Lee knew what it was to lose a partner. After hearing the whole story, maybe now she understood his desperation. "Thank you."

Lee stood from her seat and brushed off her pants, not making eye contact, "Sure. Anything to piss off Malachi."

She marched past him and Vira to the kitchen behind them. Kennex turned just enough to watch her root around as if she owned the space. Fighting like hells to save a loved one, a partner, seemed a terrible agony. Kennex wouldn't wish it on his worst enemy. The only existence that could be worse, he realized, was losing a partner then working like hells to retroactively save them in the form of someone else.

- THIRTEEN -

Kennex stood in his dorm, perched in front of the window, but the Illyarium trees could hardly be seen behind the holonotes plastered on the glass. Over the last three days, one turned to four which then spiraled into dozens and dozens of brightly colored squares in a system of organization that was more chaotic than planned. Pages of the books had been copied and thrown onto the window alongside scribbles of thoughts and fraying connections.

See-ames referred to the gods. Aether and Erebus were the two he recognized, but Lee translated the journal and found the gods were as common as constellations in the sky. The other word Malachi offered, "*eunim,*" hadn't been found yet. The lack of knowledge surrounding Stellotrian culture was a hindrance to the search. Kennex wished he had known a Stellotrian as Ari had—or he wished she had spoken about her guardian more often.

"The holoscreen addition to the window was meant for photos, you know." Lee's voice called out. Rather than turn, Kennex continued to re-read over a page he had memorized. A slim hand tapped against the window and all the holonotes fluttered away to reveal the Illyarium forest again. Kennex sighed as his and Lee's reflection came into view with it. She scoffed, "You're not even dressed."

As always, Lee was dressed to the nines. A navy blazer hung too large on her frame and was decorated in white and gold floral embroidery. It matched the pants with legs so long the hem covered the shoes she wore. Kennex wasn't sure how she glided across the floor without tripping over herself. The shirt under the blazer covered her entire chest, climbing up her neck, but had no sleeves. It also didn't reach the top of her pants revealing her bellybutton. Overdressed compared to his simple, gray sleep pants. Her black hair was pulled up into a ponytail and only exasperation existed in her violet gaze. Lee held out a wrapped sandwich.

"I've been too busy."

"Too busy to get dressed?" She snorted and Kennex gave a nod. "I don't think obsessing over old information counts as busy."

"Well, if we had new information—"

"I'm translating as quickly as I can. It's not my fault you're too dumb to learn Otri," she countered. Kennex took the sandwich with a quiet thanks. He wasn't sure if it was his Ascension or living in a resource rich region, but his appetite had grown tenfold. There wasn't a time of day where Kennex wasn't craving food. "Is that your..."

Kennex tucked a bite of the sandwich into his cheek and followed her gaze in the reflection to where she stared at his bare chest. The golden scar shimmered with his every breath. He snorted. "Yeah, it's where your buddy X'ael fraking shot me."

"I was going to call it your Ascension mark, edger."

"Ascension mark?" Kennex took another bite of his sandwich. Lee grasped the bottom of her shirt and pulled it up over her chest. He immediately sucked in a sharp breath that had him choking on his last bite. *Fraking hells*! Lee, what're you—"

His coughs and words died off when he noticed the glittering at the center of her chest. Her shapely breast band covered the more sensitive portions of her anatomy but created a bold view of her cleavage. The golden scar that matched his only elevated it. Kennex's eyes traced a vertical scar, a stab wound nearly hidden under the glow. The gold, like rays of Sol, radiated out from the scar.

"You died," he breathed.

"All Ascendants do. The last death." Lee let her shirt fall. "That's what the ascension ceremony consists of. You allow Malachi to kill you with the faith that Aether will bring you back."

Kennex stiffened when Lee raised her hand. The pads of her fingers hovered over his scar, waiting, and when he gave a curt nod, she touched him. As she felt along the raised skin hiding under the glow, her brows furrowed.

"Oh. You never said he killed you with the KSS."

Kennex didn't know X'ael's rifle had a name.

"It's not plasma. As I'm sure you realized." Lee cleared her throat. "It stands for 'Kinetic Superheated Shells' and it—it fires *metal*. Rips through its target like knives."

"Yeah. That's what it felt like," Kennex mumbled. If he lingered in the memory long enough, he heard the telltale crack of the weapon firing— like lightning. He could feel the heat of shrapnel blowing through him. Kennex took a step back and Lee's hand fell. "If you're here, let's get started. We haven't touched the last few pages of the journal yet."

"We can't today." Lee crossed her arms.

"What?"

"You have to leave the dorm, Kennex. Show your face."

"No, I don't."

Lee huffed. "You think people haven't noticed your absence? That Malachi hasn't? It's only a matter of time before he's knocking on your door, and he won't bring you breakfast like I did."

"Will he flash me then feel me up like you did?"

Her hands fell to her hips. "Don't flatter yourself, edger. Now either you put on some fraking clothes and come with me, or I drag you out half naked. I don't care either way."

"I have to figure this out," Kennex said, humor gone. He tapped the window twice so the holonotes came flying back into place. "I don't have time to play pretend for Malachi, Lee."

She pressed her lips together before speaking, "You're Ascendant now, Kennex. You have all the time in the universe."

"But Ari doesn't."

Lee held his gaze for a few seconds before looking away. Kennex hadn't figure Lee out yet. There were too many other puzzles to play with. Of the three Ascendants on his supposed fireteam, she had been the one he spent the most time with. Vira and Brin were always over at least for dinner, they brought food with them, but Lee had kept to her word and aided him in the research. They both shared an appreciation of absorbing as much knowledge as possible, and not killing one another became easier as the days wore on. Nobody was more surprised than Kennex when he realized he enjoyed Lee's presence. Other than Lee, that is. He knew this because she reminded him every other day of her shock.

"Fine," she sighed. Lee slid out of her blazer and tossed it onto the couch. "If you go with Vira and play the part of Ascendant trainee, then I will stay here and continue translating," she muttered under her breath. "My plans can be rescheduled, I suppose."

"Thank you," Kennex breathed in relief. He stepped past her, pausing halfway to his bedroom. "Wait, did you say Ascendant trainee?"

"You think you don't need training?" Lee scoffed and picked up the journal. "I, alone, have bettered you twice."

"You attacked me from behind with no warning both times."

"Oh, I'm sorry, is fighting different out in the edges of the system? Do enemies out there warn you before they attack?"

Kennex let out a disbelieving laugh. With a shake of his head, he pressed the tip of his thumb under his top teeth and flicked it out to her with gusto—the local way of expressing displeasure toward a person. An unusual custom he learned firsthand when tucking his thumb between two fingers and twisting, like he would in Outer Orbit, hadn't conjured the insult he wanted.

Lee brushed him away, nose buried in the journal, and with muttered curses Kennex got dressed for the day.

***

"ALL OF YOU ARE WRONG." KENNEX TRIED TO IGNORE THE STARES AS HE walked through the gardens outside of the dorm with Vira by his side. "I don't need training."

"I've seen your hand-to-hand combat, and it was abysmal," Vira hummed.

"Yeah," Brin jogged up and jostled his shoulders, "and I felt it. Definitely needs work."

"I broke your fraking skull, screwhead." Kennex shook him off. Brin just laughed in response. Kennex didn't spend his youth being beaten black and blue by Recluse to have these Ascendants criticize him. He had been a champion in Acheron's fighting pit more than once. He had never been as good as Ari, but that was because she was a savant of violence. Kennex didn't shine until he found his first hand cannon. Admittedly, relying on his weapon of choice may have made him rusty in other avenues, but he was a good fighter when it came down to it. Recluse wouldn't have kept him around otherwise. "I've had training. I don't need more."

Vira made the effort to push her glasses down her nose to give him a skeptical glance. "From who? That criminal perched by Wild Space? Rewind?"

"Recluse."

"Never heard of him," Brin added.

Recluse would foam at the mouth if he ever heard this conversation.

The last time Kennex cut through these gardens was for Sermon. This time, Vira and Brin steered him to the right. When the courtyard opened into a path down a set of stone steps, Kennex was startled to see the beginnings of a tight knit community. Unassuming, simple, and buzzing with life. Head-to-head with pictures of other random colonies about the system, Kennex would not have been able to pick this one out as the home for Ascendants. After passing a few storefronts, they walked into a loud, bustling market akin to the one on Acheron—though cleaner and more spacious.

"Welcome to the Commissary." Vira announced.

Stalls and booths were decorated in bright colors and a few larger, triangular tarps were locked in place overhead to provide shade from Sol. Live music drifted softly through the air and the first scent to overpower his senses was sweet.

"Bee!" Brin cheered and steered them straight to a pale blue stand, made of metal and wood and covered in potted flowers for sale. Boxes on display showcased various fruits. "Please tell me you have some apgoes."

The light skinned woman behind the booth had long, wavy blonde hair with colorful undertones of pink and blue. Her bare arms were decorated in tattoos—a mix of stationary and kinetic markings. Trees and plant life decorated most of it, but the portrait of a cat rested around her forearm with swishing tails and twitching ears. Kennex furrowed his brow as the faint ringing returned to the back of his head. Ascendant? This woman didn't seem it.

Bee twisted her lips and arched a brow at Brin. "Depends. Do you plan on paying, Brinair?"

"Well, uh, you see..." Brin rambled on.

Bee's annoyed gaze darted to Kennex, double taking with widened blue eyes. "Wait, are you Kennex Hall?"

Kennex opened his mouth, but Brin wrapped his arm around his shoulders and grinned. "Yes! This is *the* Kennex Hall, Bee! I brought him to meet *you* specifically. Told him all about your incredible booth."

"You're so full of scrap." Bee rolled her eyes. She gathered three bright red spheres from a box. It wasn't a fruit Kennex had seen before. "As a welcome to you, Kennex."

"Oh, thank you," Kennex mumbled as Brin snatched the fruit from her. She scolded him, and as they left the booth Kennex spotted Vira sliding a purple token across the booth top. "I'm confused."

Brin tossed Vira an apgo and shoved the other into Kennex's hand. It fit in his palm and was firm to squeeze. Brin pointed to it. "It's a fruit native to Illyarium, Hall. You eat it."

Brin signed "eat" in ISL, tapping his pinched fingers against his mouth, as if Kennex was a child. Kennex used the same insulting sign he gave the man's sister this morning and Brin burst into laughter.

"Not about the fraking fruit. The woman. She's Ascendant, not adherent. Right?"

"Right." Vira nodded. "Everyone here in the Commissary is Ascendant. Only very specific adherents are allowed in Haven, and they must wear their uniform."

Kennex scanned the various, unique booths. A man blowing glass in a furnace was the closest and the heat bit at the back of his neck as they passed.

"Most of the Ascendants working here have ceased mission work, but they haven't officially retired yet."

"Why?"

"Why not?" Brin bit down into the apgo and the crisp, red skin broke to reveal yellow flesh that immediately dripped down his hand. "When I retire, I'm sure as hells not going up to the Golden Halo." He nodded his head up to where the halo now rested as a golden band perpendicular to the Overflow Ring. "Bet it's so fraking boring up there."

Paradise was promised to them, it hovered overhead as a constant reminder, but they chose not to go. Kennex stared up at the Golden Halo trying to understand why anyone wouldn't choose it as a home. Vira bumped her shoulder into his. "If you haven't noticed, we have a community here. Haven was created by Ascendants and is governed by us. Sure, Malachi obviously has overarching control, but he rarely intervenes here." She bit into her fruit less messily. "We even have our own economy."

Kennex recalled the purple token. Brin snorted, "Yeah, and thanks to it I'm going to be panhandling for spare credits soon. Hall, you need to get your scrap together so we can get assigned a mission sooner rather than later." Brin began to lap at the juices on his hand. "I'm sick of being broke."

"You're sick, period." Vira blanched at his action. "Who knows where that fraking hand has been." Brin's smile widened and he opened his mouth only for Vira to shove the unbitten side of her apgo into the space. "Don't talk."

Brin mumbled something about "more for him" and returned to eating as they walked. Vira pointed out other booths of staple Ascendants he should know, and each one tried to offer him gifts. Vira turned down most, only missing the few that Brin snatched up too quick for her to deny. Kennex finally bit into his apgo and was surprised by the floral, sweet tang that coated his tongue. It was too sweet for his preference, and his first thought was of how Ari would enjoy it.

"This is the end of the Commissary." Vira paused after coming down a collection of stone steps like those that separated the dorm courtyard to the next level. "If you go left from here it'll take you to the food court and Rakerby's—it's a bar." She pointed to the right. "And that way will take you the arena. It's where Ascendants can spar and train." Kennex took a step to the right, but Vira pulled him back. "Oh, no. We're not going to the arena."

"You said I needed to train."

"We did." Vira smirked and Brin laughed. They continued straight on the path, down to the next level where Kennex spotted the golden gates of Haven's entrance. She motioned for him to follow with a wave over her shoulder. "Come on, new light. We're taking you to the Curator's Nest."

"The Curator's fraking what?"

The Curator's Nest.

A wall outside the large building—suspiciously shaped like a round nest—had the words painted bold and decorative. A mural of children with wings surrounded the title, and beneath it was a phrase.

"We grow and train in his nest, and pray to Aether that one day we may be chosen to fly," Kennex read, not hiding the judgment and disgust in his voice. "You're *fraking* kidding me."

"It's a camp where—"

"Yeah, I know what it is," Kennex interrupted Vira.

Everyone knew the well-off Yarians could send their kids to a camp where they could be trained in the hopes of one day becoming Ascendant. It wasn't a guarantee, but nobody could deny the influence.

Brin jogged ahead of them claiming to be late. He was volunteering as a counselor to help train the younger generations. Kennex would be lying if he said he didn't like Brin, but seeing the man associated with this program was off-putting. "I'm not joining a bunch of kids as they play pretend."

"You say kids, but they're about your age." Vira shrugged. "We're five years out from an Ascension ceremony so the Upper Unit are all twenty years old."

Kennex had pictured him standing at attention among a group of eleven-year-olds. This was better, and he conceded that to Vira with a grunt. She chuckled and approached the Nest. With a sigh, Kennex dragged his feet after her. Like a proper tour guide, Vira pointed out the classrooms along the interior of the building along with tiny dorms, a mess hall, and the training field in the center.

"There are three units. Lower, Middle, and Upper. Youngest we have here right now are around ten," Vira explained. "All three units live here."

They cut through a lounge area. It was filled with furniture in good conditions. Holoscreens and bookshelves lined the walls. The camp facilities were nice. Kennex and Ari would have traded vital organs to have these living conditions when they were young. A few attendees were scattered about and watched them with rapt attention.

"Did you live here?" Kennex asked.

"No. Brin and Lee did, but I didn't attend the camp," Vira replied. She offered no further explanation.

A set of double doors led them outside onto a grassy field, but the sky was blocked by a ceiling of glass. Noise surrounded them as multiple groups, led by Ascendants, trained. The groups were seemingly organized by age. Vira ushered him further onto the field where the older groups congregated.

"How long has the camp been around?" Kennex asked.

"Not too long. Couple hundred years." Vira responded. The statement was comical.

"And there's an Ascension Ceremony every five years?"

"Just about. It isn't a strict timeline. Kind of depends on who's on deck to ascend and how many openings are available. We never go over a thousand," Vira explained. The field was vast with different portions set up for various tasks—weapons, weightlifting, speed, agility. Near the back, furthest away from where they entered, Kennex recognized Brin watching them. "On average only one or two people from a unit even get chosen."

As they walked, Kennex glanced at Vira curiously. "How old are you?"

"I'm surprised it took you this long to ask."

"Haven't really thought about it until now." Kennex replied with a shrug. He didn't like thinking about their ages. It only reminded him of his own altered lifespan.

"This is actually my centennial year. It's one of the big landmarks we celebrate."

Kennex blinked in surprise. "You're a hundred years old?"

"Hundredth as an Ascendant." Vira slowed her pace as they approached the training group. "We count from the Ascension. That's why the public gets confused sometimes. I am ninety-nine right now, going on 100 in a few weeks, and you are zero."

"Zero? Seriously?"

Vira grinned and reached out to pinch his cheek. "Next year we'll celebrate your first Ascension Day like a big boy."

Kennex slapped her hand away with a chuckle, "Shut up."

They were near enough to hear soft grunts as the twenty-five attendees did crunches while lined up in rows of three. The interior wall of the field was a stone's throw away and where Brin loitered. Beside him, also leaning against the wall, was an immortal Kennex did not recognize.

"Who is that?"

"Kolche," Vira muttered. "He's an annoying son of a—"

"Vira!" Kolche greeted in a bellowing voice.

Kennex smirked as Vira mumbled a string of curses. They walked around the working attendees to the two men. Brin must have known Vira's distaste for the immortal beside him because he grinned and shot Kennex a knowing look of amusement. Kolche's attention shifted from Vira to him. "Well, well, if it isn't the Outer Orbit poser." The man's voice alone immediately irritated Kennex. "Nice to finally meet you."

"Sure," he replied.

Kolche pushed off the wall and, in the same movement, threw something. Kennex twisted in time to dodge the flying projectile, but he still felt the sting of metal as it brushed against his cheek. Vira scolded him, but Kolche just grinned.

"Well, look at that, the poser doesn't bleed."

"Told you he was the real deal," Brin bragged.

Vira sucked in a sharp breath and pushed her glasses up to pinch at the bridge of her nose. "You stupid fraking screwhead. Will you just let us do what we came here to do?"

"What? Train?" Kolche snorted. The attendees had slowed in their exercises. "The great and chosen Ascendant Kennex Hall, lifted from the darkness, wants to train with my class of children?"

Vira said they were twenty, but Kolche still referred to them as children. He supposed to an immortal, twenty was nothing. A mere blink. Depending on how old Kolche was, he wondered if the Ascendant even remembered being twenty. Kennex could. Clear as day. At twenty, Venom was well formed. Stealing credits, taking lives, and staining his hands red for Recluse. Kennex had not felt like a child.

"I'm sure they haven't worked their assess off just to have you dismiss them in a comment meant to insult me," Kennex said. He kept his irritation out of his voice best he could. The sneer Kolche responded with told him he hadn't done very well.

In a beat, amusement took hold on the immortal's features. Kennex automatically groaned as Kolche marched over to the attendees who scrambled to return to their duties. Vira shook her head from beside him.

"Fledglings!" Kolche shouted. The young men and women snapped to attention with a resounding reply. Kennex's features twisted in disbelief at the dedication to the Nest theme. "Ascendant Kennex Hall thinks he should be training with you." He turned his back to the attendees to smirk at Kennex with crossed arms. "Oh, great and powerful Ascendant of the edgers, I don't think you should be training with my class because I don't think you're at *their* level. My children will put your supposed ability to resurrect to the test."

"You just had to challenge him," Vira muttered.

Kennex shot her a glare. "I didn't challenge him. I didn't challenge anyone."

"Now," Kolche clapped his hand. "The fledgling that kills Kennex Hall first gets two feathers."

A ripple of excitement that Kennex did not grasp passed through the crowd of twenty-year-olds. Kennex leaned toward Vira, "What the hells does he mean by feathers?"

"It's a point system," Brin replied instead as he walked up from the wall to them. "Ascendants must 'earn their wings' post-Ascension and fledglings keep track of skills via metaphorical feathers."

"Earn their wings??" Kennex furrowed his brow. "What the frak does that even mean?"

"Oh, have we not talked about that yet?" Vira asked.

Kennex opened his mouth to give a resounding no, but all that passed through was a grunt of air as he was tackled to the ground. Brin's guffaw echoed as Kennex shoved off the skinny twenty-year-old that had taken him down. He was only half up when another two lunged for him. Kennex ducked under a punch, spinning at the same time, and kicked the swinger into the fledgling beside them.

A wave of bodies crashed over him in a blur of attacks, and soon he found the groove. Kennex wouldn't deny the fledglings' skill, and if he were stuck in this fight prior to Diomedes he may not have fared well. What worked for him was the lack of exhaustion. The fledglings would attack again and again, over and over, but Kennex felt as he did at the start. His limbs didn't ache, he wasn't gasping for breath, and his mind stayed sharp regardless of the number lunging for him at once. Even when a few fledglings sported blades, the attacks that found purchase created wounds that did not make him pause. A flash of pain then, glowing, he would knock the attacker aside.

He wasn't sure how long this had gone on for, but a number of the fledglings laid on the ground panting. He wasn't cruel—he wasn't Recluse. Kennex didn't fight to incapacitate, only stun and exhaust. Another punch was swung at his head and as he leaned out of the way, he spotted it. Not a window to slip away and escape this nonsense, but an accident in full motion.

A female fledgling was rushing forward to drive her knife into his neck at the same time a male one rushed to tackle him. They would collide. The blade would end up in a body that would bleed.

He twisted and rushed to meet the young man halfway. The fledgling's gray eyes blew wide as he tried to scramble back, but Kennex grabbed him roughly—in time for the other fledgling's dagger to bury into his own shoulder. Kennex grunted and threw his elbow back into the young woman's face. She collapsed.

"Enough!" He dropped the fledgling he saved. The entire field stilled at his voice, but Kennex turned to find Kolche. He stood by the wall with

Vira and Brin. Directly behind them was glass paneling that viewed into one of the indoor lounges. "That fledgling," he spat the term out mockingly, "could've been killed. This is over."

Kolche rolled his eyes. "He would've been fine. Worst case scenario we call a medic."

"That wouldn't have helped anything if that blade ended up in his heart!"

"It's a risk of training. They all understand that." Kolche shrugged then waved a finger at him with a grin. "Honestly, you're better than I thought you'd be, Hall. You have plenty to learn, but we can officially scratch off 'survived twenty-five mortals' off your list." He tilted his head. "Well, maybe."

Kennex furrowed his brow, but a searing pain interrupted his berating of Kolche. Kennex choked on air as an energy blade pierced through his back and out the front. It deactivated in a blink, but left him with a gaping, glowing hole in his torso. He grabbed his abdomen, attempting to stem blood that was not there, and glanced over his shoulder to spot the sheepish grimace of the fledgling he had saved.

Kennex landed in the grass. Kolche was clapping and shouting something, but his eyes focused on figures beyond the Ascendants staring him. Inside the lounge, sitting on a couch against the furthest wall, was Malachi. Kennex's fading mind registered the leader, but it did not recognize the woman sitting by him. Older, hair so blonde it appeared white, and sharp, blue eyes that burned into him even from this distance.

Kennex blinked and it was all gone.

- FIFTEEN -

Kennex decided he didn't mind dying if it meant he got to spend a second with the memory of Ari. He recognized her, leaning against a pillar, with her eyes cast up to the sky. It was unheard of for them to go this long without talking. Kennex felt like he was missing a part of himself.

Life would be easier if fate had taken a limb from him rather than part of his soul.

He took his time approaching her. His hesitation born from fear that he'd find the mimic where she stood. As Kennex settled beside her, he felt relief. This was Ari.

"What do you think about when you look at the stars?" The memory of Ari whispered.

He remembered this. The sleep cycle prior to their first job as task runners, Kennex had woken in a too quiet room to find she had slipped out of their shared home. He found her standing alone in the Atrium—gazing up through the thick glass into the expanse of space.

"That there are too many of them," Kennex answered. Her lips twitched up, but she didn't look his way. Kennex asked the question he already knew the answer to just to hear her voice. "Why are you up right now, Ari?"

"I had a bad dream," she murmured. *"I was trapped again—in the metal.*

I haven't had that nightmare in years." Kennex remained silent, waiting on bated breath for her to finally look his way. Despite knowing it was coming, when she turned her head, Ari's gaze still knocked the breath from his lungs. *"Do you think once we start exploring out there... I'll feel less trapped?"*

Kennex remembered his answer all too clearly.

No. As long as we're under Recluse's thumb, we'll always be trapped.

It was so stupid to say.

Kennex had been upset they were taking a job as task runners rather than just leaving. Still, it gave him no excuse to say those words when she was clearly seeking comfort. Rather than repeat his mistake, Kennex lifted his hand and let it ghost over the memory of her cheek. He swallowed, but the lump in his throat didn't budge. "Yes. You were born to be among the stars, Ari. Some of our favorite days are gonna be off this broken barge and out there."

But, the comfort was given far too late, and those weren't the words she took to heart.

Ari turned her head to look back at the stars, phasing through his hand into a fine mist, and Kennex watched her disappear.

- SIXTEEN -

Kennex wasn't a fan of stars, but Ari's love for them clued him into what was missing.

He jumped out of bed, legs tangling in the sheets, and stumbled out the room. Lee was in the kitchen, and she turned just as he barreled in.

"*Aether*!" She stood at the kitchen island with a plate of cut fruit and the journal open. "What is your hurry?"

"Diamond." Kennex closed the space between them. "How do you say diamond? Or—Or how do you spell it—"

"D-I-A-M—" It wasn't Lee who spoke.

Kennex's head snapped to the couches where his last murderer sat. His eyes narrowed. "You."

Lee let out a slow sigh and motioned to the fledgling who offered an awkward wave. "Kennex, this is Tryptan. He wanted to apologize—"

"I am *so* sorry, Ascendant Hall." Tryptan stood, hands up in surrender. "What you did for me was great, and I stabbed you in the back," Tryptan winced at his own words. "I am really sorry, but I needed those feathers."

Kennex vaguely recalled the feathers and 'earning wings.' He blinked a few times then waved off the fledgling to focus back on his point. "Diamond, Lee. I need—"

She uttered the word in Otri, and he nodded.

"Yeah. How do you spell that? Or better yet," Kennex jabbed his finger on the open page a few times, "find it. I need you to find it."

"Kennex, what are you—"

"*Eunim.* We've been scouring those damned book for the word *eunim*, but obviously it's not there," Kennex gasped. "But the stars—the constellations. I saw a bunch of constellations right before Malachi killed me, but there was one in particular that stuck with me."

A thoughtful look filled her violet eyes as her lips twisted. She finally sighed. "The journal said the *see-ames* were as common as constellations in the sky, but maybe my translation wasn't as..."

Lee didn't finish her thought and instead dove into the journal.

Kennex sucked in a deep breath and rubbed the back of his neck. He grimaced as his hand found a cold sweat, and he wiped the dampness on his shirt.

"So, I don't know what's going on." Tryptan drew his words out.

Kennex glanced back to him. "You're still here?"

"Well, yeah, it's been like eleven seconds since I last spoke." Tryptan shrugged. He squirmed in place. The young man's features were so open that Kennex could read every emotion flashing in the fledgling's gray eyes. His training gear had been replaced with a plain, dark jacket and matching pants. "Ascendant Hall—"

"Don't call me that. It's just Kennex." He paused, taking a deep breath. "Look, it's fine. You did what you had to do, and I get that." Tryptan's face split in a wide grin. Awkward nerves turning to relieved excitement. Kennex cleared his throat. "You can—"

"Here," Lee blurted.

All attention diverted back to the journal.

"When I was scanning for *see-ames* or *eunim,* I remember seeing references to diamonds a few times, but most were referring to crystals," Lee explained. She pointed to a passage on the page. "This is the only time it's referenced as a constellation."

"Okay. Good." Kennex frowned when Lee seemed worried. "Not good?"

"It doesn't give us a lot," Lee replied. "It's basically just the author saying he feels blessed because his constellation is overhead. He describes the diamond shape with reverence—almost worship. It just goes on and on then ends with him wanting to be closer to Aether." Lee flipped a page with a huff. "Then it rattles on about Aether for like two pages. It's *obsessive*."

Kennex rubbed his face and slumped forward to lean against the counter with a groan.

"So," he thought aloud, "assuming the constellation I remember wasn't a coincidence—"

"I sincerely doubt anything involving Malachi can be called a coincidence."

"Then maybe the constellation itself is named *eunim*?"

"That would follow along with the *see-ames* being as common as constellations," Lee agreed. "Otradu's constellations are their gods? I don't know much about Stellotrian religion."

Neither did Kennex. Again, he wished he had the journal Ari had stolen for him. He didn't recall a mention of *see-ames*, but at the time he was reading it, Kennex hadn't known what to look for.

"Why don't you guys ask a Stellotrian what it means? They should know right?" Tryptan chimed in. As attention focused on him, the fledgling squirmed in place and offered an anxious smile. "Right?"

Lee raised an eyebrow. "You're still here?"

"Yes—"

"Even if you don't count the court itself, we're in Sector One of Illyarium," Kennex replied. "The chances of running into a Stellotrian here are less than low."

Tryptan shrugged. "Yeah, but, Kharees is right next door." He pointed over his shoulder for emphasis. "If you use the Expressway, it takes only a couple hours to get there." Kennex glanced to Lee who didn't seem surprised by this information, but Tryptan continued to ramble, "In the Epsilon Quadrant of Upolent—or maybe it was the Chi Quadrant—no, no. It was Epsilon because Tawny said her family had a vacation home around there. Anyways, they have the Magus Market. A bunch of Stellotrians live there."

"Magus Market?" Kennex hadn't heard of a collection of Stellotrians in Upolent. He looked to Lee for confirmation. "This true?"

"Okay, yes, but—"

"And you didn't think to tell me?" Kennex blurted. "We've been struggling through this journal and there's a Stellotrian community right next door?" Lee tried to speak, but he added, "How could you not suggest this as an idea? We could've had—"

Lee groaned. "Aether, will you shut up? I didn't suggest it because I don't make a habit of suggesting bad ideas." Kennex tried to cut in, but she pointed at him. "No Stellotrian community is keen on letting outsiders in—let alone fraking Ascendants. What do you think would happen if you strolled in demanding answers?"

"Lee—"

"And I don't appreciate you taking a tone with me, edger." She threw her hands up with a frown. "I've gone above and beyond for you in this search. I basically live in your dorm these days rummaging through the few resources we have. I can recite parts of that damned journal from memory."

Kennex squeezed the back of his neck, trying to loosen the tension, and sighed, "I'm sorry, okay?" He paced to his sink to pour a glass of water. "I'm just frustrated."

Lee's glare softened.

Tryptan cleared his throat, "Can I ask what this is all this about?" They both looked at him. He sighed, "And yes, I am still here."

Before Kennex could brush off the young man, the door opened, and Vira strolled in with Brin a step behind her. They both held boxes of food. She nodded in greeting. "Oh, good. You're still here, Tryptan. Come grab this."

Tryptan rushed over to take the box from her and Kennex trailed behind him. While the fledgling carried the box into the kitchen with Brin, Kennex shot Vira a glare. "Is there a reason why he's here?"

"Yeah, I invited him." Vira turned but paused when Lyris came in carrying two bags. "Here let me—" As Vira attempted to take the bags, Lyris brushed her away with a chuckle and greeted Kennex before breezing into his kitchen as well. He gave Vira an expectant look that she laughed at. "Relax. Tryptan wanted to apologize for what happened, and I wanted to feed him something other than the meals they get at camp—as a reward."

"A reward for killing me?"

"You let him." Vira clapped his arm, shaking him in place.

"I didn't—" Kennex's words fell flat as Vira left him.

He blew out a breath then tossed back the water he had left in his glass. Standing in his dorm's open foyer, staring into the kitchen, Kennex watched a familiar but unrecognizable scene unfold. Lyris had shed from her mask and rolled up her black sleeves to open the boxes of food. Lee dug out plates from his cabinets as Vira grabbed bottles of brew and water from the fridge. Brin loudly shared some story with Tryptan, who clung to his every word, as he ignored his sister who was scolding him to help.

Dinner looked like this most nights.

Tryptan was new and Lyris didn't often make it, but dinner was an event. It didn't feel out of place for him. Kennex still struggled with the concept. The busiest evening meals he used to have were the few times Ari and him would eat at the Barrel surrounded by other denizens of Acheron. Kennex enjoyed this. It was what he always craved without admitting, but that thought filled him with unbearable guilt. Here he was awaiting food in an atmosphere that was warm, light, and inviting.

Kennex wondered where Ari would fit among this crew—if she'd set aside prejudice against Ascendants to give them a chance. Lee glanced across the dorm to meet his gaze and she tilted her head in question. The stiffness of his spine and coiled tension in his chest loosened with every step he took closer to the kitchen, but the guilt weighed heavier.

"We need to go to Upolent," Lee chimed when he settled beside her. She pushed a plate of food into his hands. The entire group huddled around the island eating. Lyris and Tryptan sat in two of the three barstools pushed up against the countertops. "Epsilon Quadrant."

Vira snorted, "Yeah? Okay. While we're at it, let's vacation in Caegra too, hmm?"

"Hells yeah. Can we? That animal attack closed the zoo, but the Hall of Mirrors is still open," Brin added with a mouthful of food.

Lee slapped the bottom of his chin, making her twin snicker and swat her away. "I'm being serious. We're not getting any further with the information we have. If we had some context to go along with the journals, if we knew who wrote them, then maybe, but right now it's impossible. Upolent offers us a larger source of information to draw from."

"What's in Upolent that will help?" Lyris asked.

"Stellotrians," Kennex answered.

Brin paused, jaw slack, and Lyris squirmed in her seat as her eyes went to her plate.

Vira, however, let out a loud groan while rubbing her face with her hands. "Frak! I just knew you were going to say something stupid like that."

Kennex wanted to offer their argument, but Lee shot him a look from the corner of her eye and her hand briefly brushed against his. A warning. He kept quiet.

When Vira dropped her hands, her gaze was one of exhaustion. "Are you insane? Let's say I get permission for us to leave the court. I find a job in Upolent, and I convince Malachi to let it be the new light's first mission—"

"Perfect cover." Lee shrugged.

"Even if all that went over well," Vira stabbed a fork into her food with a questionable amount of force, "What makes you think a Stellotrian will talk to any of us Ascendants?"

Kennex set his hands on the counter. "Sure, Vira, you're recognizable as an Ascendant, but we—" Lee hummed and shook her head when Kennex met her gaze. "What?"

"You didn't tell him? You have this grand plan, and you didn't tell him?" Vira chuckled in exasperation. She turned to face him directly. "The second you step foot into Upolent they will know you're an Ascendant. *Everyone* will know. We get flagged."

"What?" Kennex's eyes widened. "How?"

"The spark," Tryptan groaned. "Oh, Aether, I totally forgot about Pulse."

"What the hells are all of you talking about?" Kennex grunted.

Brin was in the process of refilling his plate as Vira and Lee glared at one another, so it was Lyris who cleared her throat and spoke up. "Pulse is what the locals call Upolent's spark." The mentions of a spark brought back memories of the cat on Diomedes. Or 'not cat', he supposed. "It's ingrained in all Upolent's systems and runs the city. It monitors the population, and it can recognize Ascendants."

"Seriously?" Kennex leaned against the counter. "How? How does it run a city as large as Upolent while also monitoring its population close enough to tag Ascendants? Do Ascendants have some notable signature it can—"

"One question at a time, new light. *Aether*," Vira scoffed.

Kennex felt his cheeks warm and pushed off the counter to stand rather than lean. He cleared his throat.

Tryptan bounced in his seat. "Nobody knows the actual mechanism because the Khareesian engineers keep it real close to their chest, but there are rumors that it's able to read the light energy in an Ascendant's body and *that's* what triggers it."

Vira rapped her knuckles against the counter. "I don't care how it works, it just does. Your plan is flawed, and there isn't a Stellotrian in Upolent that's going to cooperate with us."

"Fine." Lee crossed her arms. "Then we take the fledgling too."

Tryptan's eyes widened comically followed by a bright grin. Vira simply scoffed, "Oh, great. So now I'm trying to convince Malachi to let the new light *and* a fledgling leave the court. Fantastic."

"There's no other option," Lee argued. "Stellotrian or not, there isn't a single soul in Upolent that would help an Ascendant regardless of the credits we offer. That means we need outside help. The two mortals already clued in are right here." She motioned to Lyris and Tryptan who both straightened in their seats. "There's no way in hells Malachi is allowing an adherent out of the court, but he *has* allowed fledglings out on the rare occasion."

"Emphasis on the word rare," Vira snorted. She scratched the back of her head, just under where her tight bun sat, and sighed. "So, this is our scrap of a plan then? Get to Upolent?"

Kennex glanced around the counter as resolve settled in place and his lips twitched up into a smirk. He gave Vira a tight nod. She groaned again.

Brin drummed his fingers against the counter before pumping a fist. "Frak yeah! Mission time." He tilted his head then pointed to Kennex who raised an eyebrow at the motion. "We seriously need to kill you."

"What?"

"If we go on mission and you die, I'm not carrying your unconscious body around waiting for you to wake up." Brin shrugged. The other eyes at the table drifted to stare at him, and Kennex slumped against the island counter. He had a bad feeling he was going back to the Curator's Nest.

- SEVENTEEN -

Kennex would never admit it aloud, but he had learned some new tricks these last two weeks in the Curator's Nest. Not from the screwhead Kolche who had taken to mocking him from a distance while training fledglings. Kennex understood why Vira hated him.

What he learned came directly from Lee, Brin, and Vira. Though he had fared well against the fledglings, fighting Ascendants was a different beast. For the first few days, the three of them wiped the floor with Kennex every time. It didn't help that the style was unusual. They fought, and in turn taught him to fight, in a purely offensive manner. There was no care for their bodies, no caution to injury, and the realization made perfect sense to him.

"Frak." Kennex grunted as his back slammed into the hard ground. Lee stood a few feet away spinning her chain with a grin. He pushed onto his elbows and blew out a breath. "This is hardly fair."

"How so? Because I'm using my weapon?" Lee asked. Kennex rose back into a ready position and motioned to himself as proof to the imbalance. She dropped the bladed chain and it dematerialized into nothing. Lee tightened her ponytail and slid into ready position herself. "Edger, if you think that was the only reason I was kicking your ass I have bad news for you."

With a grunt, he lunged forward to attack.

Kennex had sparred Ari before. Not enough to learn from her, but enough to recognize that Lee fought *very* differently. It wasn't even the inability for Lee to die that made them different because Ari had a bad habit of fighting like she couldn't die either. Ari was an unstoppable, runaway train barreling into someone at full speed. Lee was like a river pulling someone under in harsh currents they could not beat—Lee was fluid.

It was what made blocking her attacks so difficult.

He kept his punches in succession to try and avoid giving her the time to retaliate, but Lee found it regardless. Kennex swung his leg in a roundhouse kick that did not land. As soon as his foot returned to the ground, she was climbing up him. Her foot pushed off his thigh, hands on his shoulders, and in a blink she was swinging around his body. The momentum threw him to the ground.

"You're still doing it," Lee hissed.

"Doing what?" Kennex huffed and pushed back to his feet.

"Fighting for someone else."

"What does that even mean?"

Kennex had only been on his feet a second when she lunged at him. He tried to catch her but she spun, placing her back to him, and elbowed him in the gut. Doubled over, she grabbed him around the neck and used her weight to flip him over her shoulder. As his back hit the ground, his teeth sunk into his lower lip. Finally broken of the habit, Kennex didn't wipe his arm across his mouth searching for blood. He rolled over and glared at her. She kept her hands on her hips and stared down at him. "You fight like there's somebody beside you to watch out for." Kennex locked his jaw. "That's what leaves you open for these attacks. Instead of focusing on the fight, you're distracted by protecting someone who isn't there."

"Is it so bad that I would be looking out for whoever was with me?" Kennex scoffed.

"Yes, because it's fraking stupid." Lee replied. "You're an *Ascendant*. The people you're fighting beside can't die. They don't need you to protect them."

Kennex yanked on her ankle roughly. Her arms pinwheeled for a second before she fell back onto her ass. Hand still on her ankle, he dragged her closer while lunging at her just as she tried to sit up. Kennex pinned her by the shoulders. "Now who was distracted?"

"My point still stands, screwhead," Lee hissed. Her hands moved quick, a blur of motion, and suddenly he was being flipped onto his back with a grunt. She peered down at him. "How good of a partner could Lucky Fox have been if you were constantly having to babysit her in a fight?"

Kennex shoved her to the side, and they ended up rolling over one another four times before he landed on top of her again. "Don't talk about something you know nothing about. Ari is the best fighter I've ever seen. Sometimes she'd just get carried away. I *liked* watching her back."

"Why wouldn't you, edger?" Lee wrapped her legs around his waist and hooked her arms under his to roll him over her head. It ended with him on his back with her on top of him—knees pressing into his neck sitting on his chest as he clawed at her thighs. "Your entire life all you've ever been is her shadow. Now you finally have the chance to stand out, to be something great, and you won't fraking take it."

In her rant she leaned back, and he wrapped his right leg on her left shoulder to twist her off him. Lee grunted when her side hit the ground and he pushed up to lunge at her. Lee rolled onto her front to try and jump up, but Kennex wrapped his arm around her neck in headlock. Lee struggled, but he turned his arms to break her neck. The snapping of bone shocked him back into the moment. Kennex dropped her body and scrambled back.

He couldn't tear his gaze away from the blank violet eyes boring into him. It lasted a second. In a flash of gold light, she was back. Amusement and pride shimmered in her conscious gaze and Kennex breathed a sigh of relief. Lee sat up with a broad grin, "*Finally*, edger. I've been waiting for you to kill me."

"You're insane." Kennex rubbed his face and fell back while stretching his arms out beside him. Directly overhead, the Golden Halo could be seen through the skylight. "You're absolutely out of your fraking mind."

"Maybe, but I meant what I said." Lee stretched her leg out to nudge his side with her foot. Kennex sat back up with a frown. "You're not her backup anymore. You're an equal. Maybe more."

"Ari has never considered me less than," Kennex said softly. "She's *always* considered us equals."

"If that's true then good for you." Lee shrugged. "I just know in a partnership, whether they want to admit it or not, there's always a lead." Kennex shook his head unwilling to argue this point further. Lee pressed on, "If you had actually been the lead, would the two of you have searched Diomedes for what would end up being your doom?"

Kennex stiffened as the thought settled in his mind. Maybe—No. He shook his head. He hadn't spent a lot of time thinking in terms of leader and follower. That was never their relationship. They made decisions together. Diomedes had been an outlier of mistakes made by them both. Lee stood and stretched her arms over her head. Kennex's eyes automatically followed the curve of her body.

A sharp whistle startled him, and Kennex glanced over to see Vira standing at the entrance of the training field. She motioned for them to come. Kennex looked back to Lee who held a hand out to him.

"We good?" Lee squirmed in place, an action he didn't see often from her.

"Yeah." Kennex grabbed her hand to let her pull him to his feet, but halfway up he yanked her to the ground as he rose. He grinned down at her. "We're good."

Lee laughed an insult at him and tried to kick out his knee. He jogged away, but slowed so she could catch up. Vira waited outside the camp for them. Her arms were crossed, and she shook her head at their arrival.

"Finally."

"We had you waiting like two minutes, V," Lee scoffed.

Vira's eyes dragged to Kennex. "We got the mission in Upolent."

"That's good. Isn't it?" he replied, glancing at Lee for her approval and she nodded once. "Right?"

"It is, but it comes at a cost," Vira said. Her stoicism broke into a smirk, and Kennex narrowed his eyes at her. She made a cutting motion with her fingers and Lee laughed. Kennex suddenly wished he was back in the Nest getting his ass kicked.

"This is so fraking stupid," Kennex hissed.

"Being an Ascendant means keeping up appearances," Vira called from across the room. He felt another snip of the scissors and sharpened his glare in her direction. She offered him a thumbs up.

Kennex muttered, "I like my hair long."

"Oh?" Vira heard his complaints. "That hairstyle was a conscious choice? I thought you lost a bet." Kennex cursed and she chuckled again. "There were bits of it that are uneven for crying out loud. If this is our only cost for leaving the court, I think we're lucky."

Kennex began to argue, but the stylist working on his hair hushed him and asked him to sit still. Unwilling to have a portion of his head accidentally shaved because of his irritation, Kennex steeled his posture and settled on just glaring at Vira.

He was stuck in the seat for another fifteen minutes and only moved one other time—when the buzzing of an electric razor went off by his ear. Otherwise, Kennex behaved. He saw Vira's logic. If this was all Malachi asked in return for letting them take a mission in Upolent then certainly he could pay. When the session was finished, the stylist brushed loose hair from his shoulders and spun his chair around.

It took Kennex a second to react. His hair had never been this short. The sides were shaved neatly with the only length being left at the top though even that was shorter than before. He tilted his head left to right, trying to get accustomed to the lessened weight. He rubbed at the back of his head, but frowned when his fingers didn't tangle in hair.

"Looks nice." Vira's reflection appeared over his shoulder. "I like it."

Kennex tore his gaze away from himself and huffed, "Are we done then?"

"No. But you'll like this part a lot more." Vira motioned for him to follow, and he tossed the stylist a mumbled thanks. The building she had taken him to sat on the level before the Commissary. She led him down a hall and up a set of stairs. "I had the Welder make you a new pauldron and vambrace. We had him use your old gear as a comparison."

Kennex's eyes widened. "What?"

"You need gear if we go out of the court. Do you have any new preferences you may want added? Your old gear didn't have much."

"Where is my old gear?"

"Trashed," Vira answered and held a door open for him. He stepped through into a large lab. The tables and walls were covered in metal parts, weapons, and tools. In the corner sat a forge built into the wall. "Even if the chest didn't have a hole blown through it, the gear was ancient. When was your last update?"

"Uh," he fumbled with his words, "a while ago."

Anytime they had credits for upgrades he pushed it into Ari's gear. Hers having the shield programming meant it needed better upkeep than his simple suit.

An older man came out of the back room dressed like an adherent. However, his black uniform was leathered and his mask had a built-in filter meant for metal work.

"Ascendant Kennex Hall," Vira announced.

The man, with wiry gray hair and deep age lines, set a box on the only table in the room that wasn't overcrowded with material.

Kennex walked up, Vira a step behind, and the man nodded once. "Thank you." The Welder drifted away to continue his work. "His family has been building Ascendant gear for generations. His father built me my first set when I ascended, but this Welder took the business around my fortieth year or so."

Kennex opened the box as she spoke, and he sucked in a sharp breath at the expensive material. The metal was mostly white with black and gold trim. The straps made of thick, brown leather. It shimmered in the light as Kennex titled his head to admire it and he realized the white held an unusual crisscrossing pattern that could only be seen at an angle.

"The metal is forged with crystals from Pykail," Vira answered his unasked question. "Since you're a tier one Ascendant, you get the good stuff—crushed and treated topaz from Urrhali."

"I thought Urrhali couldn't be mined," Kennex asked halfheartedly, still mesmerized by the gear. "It's too, uh, too deep and protected by the natives."

Vira chuckled. "Yeah. The Urrhali born Kaili protect this scrap with their life. They use their topaz as a weapon or tool or something. All I know is it takes a fight to get, but it makes the strongest gear. They pick up a charge in the light."

"Why would an Ascendant need such good quality gear?" Kennex asked and picked up the heavy pauldron. He pulled it onto his right shoulder and strapped it around his torso. It covered his arm from elbow to neck where it curled up into a half collar. "We can't bleed or die."

Vira shrugged. "It looks nice. The topaz will glitter when you're standing outside."

As Kennex adjusted the pauldron, Vira picked up the vambrace and held it out for him to slide his arm in. The metal sealed around his forearm and the clean, unmarred glass came to life. He chuckled and moved his arm to test the range of motion. Nothing was hindered. The gear sat heavy, but it was a weight he recognized. What wasn't familiar to him was how snug and shaped it was to his form. He investigated the box for the rest and frowned.

"Where are my boots?"

"Don't need them." Vira tapped her finger against the pauldron. "This pauldron houses the full suit. You don't need any other pieces."

"And my helmet anchor?"

"Ascendants at our level don't wear helmets, new light," Vira chuckled. "There's more power in showing our faces than hiding." Kennex let out a breathless chuckle at the claim. He spent most of his life hiding his face behind Venom's sigil, showing it now almost felt wrong. She called out another thanks to the Welder and left. Kennex jogged after her.

"If you need a heads up display to keep track of your gear stats or for aiming, we can get you something." She tapped the side of her orange tinted glasses. "That's what these are for, but you can also get your irises altered to house it."

Kennex shook his head. "Pass. I've seen X'ael's eyes."

"In defense of the tech, he specifically chose the creepiest version of it."

"I don't need it anyway." The hallway they walked down wrapped around the building and Vira seemed content to walk the length of it to get to wherever they were going. "My old heads-up display didn't have the autocorrecting sights that connected with hand cannons."

Vira glanced at him, her voice shocked, "You were aiming with just your own sight then?" He nodded. "Hmm, impressive. I only ever knew one other person who could fire successfully without the aid."

"Are they an Ascendant?"

"They were," Vira replied cryptically. They reached a door, and Kennex had no time to seek further clarification on her vague response. The room they stepped into was set up as a broadcasting site. Kennex recognized the glowing sphere of a camera hovering in the air. A woman with a headset that projected a holoscreen over her eyes stood off to the side working on a tablet. "Last bit of the deal."

Kennex shot her a heated look. "He wants me on camera?"

"There are plenty of rumors about you, but not many answers," Vira replied. "The Curator needs to control the narrative. Besides, you should thank me. I shot down the interview and recommended just some routine footage."

Kennex was thankful hearing that. The closest he had ever come to being interviewed were the few times an enforcer would catch up to him and Ari. Those interviews had a very different goal and energy. The words did give him pause though.

He turned to face Vira head on. "How come he listened to you?"

"What do you mean?"

"You convinced him to let us take a mission in Upolent. You convinced him away from an interview."

"Yeah, and?"

"How?" Kennex repeated the initial question with force. "Why does he trust you?"

"It's not trust, new light." Vira crossed her arms. "It's strategy. We've already had this conversation." She discreetly nodded to the other body in the room. "We can circle back on it later."

Not appeased, but mollified, Kennex dragged his feet to the woman with a frown. She quickly bowed to him, and his frown deepened in disgust. "Please don't."

"I'm sorry, sir?" She lifted her head again. Vira coughed behind them and he glanced over his shoulder to see her shooting a warning look. Kennex sighed and waved his hand to motion for them to move on. The woman was chubby with long, red hair wrapped intricately in a braid around the back of her head. Her pretty smile half hidden behind the holoscreen. She ushered him to a small circular step up from the ground. "If you could please stand here and activate your suit."

He hummed and played with his vambrace while walking up the ledge. The settings were all at default so Kennex would have to adjust his preferences later. Finding the activation key, he initiated the start, and the pauldron began to stretch and grow around him. The metal moved smoothly and without any hiccups or snatches in the joints. When it fully formed around him, Kennex gave himself a glance over with eyebrows raised. Ascendants had the best gear in the system, and the Welder's work was a testament to that fact.

"All right, now if you'd just look straight ahead and smile, I can snag a minute or two of footage to use." She tapped on her tablet and the camera spun around him once before ending up in front of him. Kennex stared directly into the lens. After a beat, the woman hummed. "Oh, um, Ascendant Hall?"

"Yeah?"

"If I could have you maybe not look directly into the camera? Just off to the side. And please smile."

Kennex let his eyes drag lazily to the right of the camera and sighed. Another beat passed and the woman shifted in place as she worked on her tablet. He glanced at her to see her gnawing on her lower lip, eyebrows furrowed.

"For Aether's sake, just fraking smile, new light," Vira snapped. The woman jumped but kept her head down. Kennex met Vira's eyes and she shot him a mocking grin while pointing to her own features. Annoyed, he pasted the requested smile on his face. Vira pinched the bridge of her nose. "Thank Aether I didn't let Lee be your escort, she would've killed you by now."

"I *am* smiling."

"That wasn't a smile."

"What would you call it then?"

"A grimace? A glare? Hells, call it whatever you want, but it wasn't a smile."

Kennex rubbed the back of his neck. He didn't want the camera on him. In fact, he spent his life avoiding them. Standing on a stage with one aimed at him sounded like the physical embodiment of his nightmares rather than reality. He closed his eyes in hopes that'd he'd wake up in his bed. If he were truly lucky, he'd wake up on Acheron beside Ari.

"Hey," Vira's close voice made him snap his eyes open. She stood in front of him and laid a hand on his shoulder. "You good? What's going on?"

Kennex shook his head and prayed she couldn't feel the heat radiating off his cheeks. "Nothing," he snapped. "I just don't wanna do this. What's so hard to understand about that?" Lee's earlier words about him hiding in Ari's shadow suddenly returned. "Just back off, okay?"

She held her hands up in surrender. "Fine." Vira took a step back but paused. "This is the last hurdle, new light." Kennex swallowed the thick lump that had formed in his throat. "You do this and we're on our way to Upolent tomorrow. You get your answers."

Vira stepped off the ledge and offered the woman reassurance. Kennex took in a slow, steadying breath. He always said he'd be willing to do anything to protect Ari. Technically, smiling for a camera fell under that classification, and it was the simplest fraking task. He readjusted his stance and straightened his shoulders to stand tall.

Kennex wondered what Ari would say if she saw him right now. Anger was her knee jerk reaction to anything that confused her, but he didn't think she'd be angry with him. If Ari was standing by the doorway rather than Vira, she'd probably be mocking him. Aether knew he'd never live this down. The next worst thing would be the creation of a mural.

"I've seen you crawl across glass with a hole in your hand to reach your hand cannon just so you could shoot a ruguru and piss him off further." Ari's laugh rang through his head, clear as a bell. He could imagine himself sitting in the Barrel telling this story to Trig and his partner between drinks.

"And you're telling me shooting the camera a smile is what beats you?"

Kennex chuckled under his breath and cast his gaze to the right of the camera as he stepped out of his body and lived in his head. The real tragedy of Ari not being here by his side was the loss of her untimely humor and snide remarks.

What he wouldn't give to hear her mock the Court of Aether.

- EIGHTEEN -

Being as they'd be going to Upolent in the morning, Brin suggested they kill him enough that his body wouldn't shut down from the shock of a resurrection. Just in case.

Kennex had died a few times in the span of the two weeks training, but he asked for them to spread the deaths apart. They conceded. Kennex never admitted that it was because he was afraid to lose these precious few moments in his head. What he was learning though, was it didn't change things. No matter the amount of time he was down he got to spend a minute here with a memory. It was the biggest relief he felt since learning that Ari hadn't perished on Diomedes.

Kennex sat on the stone, back to a pillar, and a younger version of Ari used the meat of his thigh as her pillow. This memory was only three of four years old. In it, they were hiding in their stash house, lounging on the couch, waiting for Recluse to get back to them about an upcoming job. Ari rested while Kennex read aloud from a book.

In this recreation, Kennex didn't need to read.

He could stare down and re-memorize features he knew by heart.

"You'd love my dorm," Kennex murmured, his words falling on deaf ears. "It's ridiculous and an insane amount of space for one person, but it's nice. The shower is life changing." He tried to rake his fingers through her hair, but they fazed through like a mist. "Met some people. I think you'd like them. Well, most of them. There's a woman named Lee." Kennex chuckled. "The two of you would either get along really well, or you'd try to kill one another."

Ari's eyes fluttered open, and he was mesmerized. She had complained about her eye color once—called it boring. It left Kennex baffled. Boring was the last word he'd use to describe any aspect of Ari. Especially her eyes. They reminded him of light passing through a glass of Acheron liquor, of the warmth from her skin as he wrapped her hands with tape, of the comfort that came as they laid side by side whispering stories to chase away nightmares. Her eyes were home.

Ari teased him when she asked him about his favorite color.

She truly couldn't fathom why he replied with "brown" so quickly.

"Can you read a book not about—" Ari's words disappeared as she did.

Kennex's eyes widened in alarm as he searched for her.

"Do you only recall memories of her?" It was Lee. She passed him, her stride casual and confident, and Kennex followed. Eventually, the figure paused and turned around to face him. If this was the mimic that lived in his head, it was doing a very good job at pretending to be Lee. Kennex searched for a mistake. "It's like she's in every single memory you have."

"She's in all the ones that matter," Kennex replied. Eyebrows furrowing when he found she was a perfect copy.

A soft lullaby drifted through the air, and he tensed. It was one he knew by heart. The tune may as well have been carved into his soul. Lee looked to her left and Kennex studied her profile for a second more.

Finally, unable to resist any longer, he turned.

Standing in one of the overgrown gardens, under the glow of Sol's rays, was a woman. Her clothing a mix of rags and cloth found and sewn together. The material so thin he could see the purple glow of nether under her sleeves. The woman held a toddler in her arms. The young boy slept with his head pressed to her chest. She sang under her breath to him. In his head, the song melded with the steady beat of her heart.

"Send her away," he whispered.

"Why? This is a happy memory," Lee responded. "It's filled with only love."

"It hasn't been a happy memory since I was eleven," Kennex hissed. "*Send her away.*"

There was no memory of his mother that wasn't tainted with pain. Every thought of her left him with the taste of blood in his mouth an ache in his chest.

Kennex's mother had been a lot of things, and the worst of them was selfish.

Even before she drove that knife into his belly, he always felt like a burden. Kennex always came second to the nether. It was a bad day for them when she'd have to spend money on food rather than more of that purple powder. No child should have to fight for attention from their mother. Kennex couldn't even remember the color of her eyes. All he could recall was the purple glow.

"She *loved* you."

"She tried to kill me." Kennex's chest tightened as his breaths came quick. "She nearly did." The scar on his abdomen burned hot as the memory of searing pain and blood-soaked fear took the forefront of his mind.

The scene shifted.

Sol's golden light dimmed, and the garden filled with shadows. The figure of his mother turned to face him. Her eyes glowed the same color of her arms and the toddler she once held with care had been replaced with a blade. "Send her away."

Too many fingers clutched around the hilt of the knife.

Too many teeth in her cruel, elongated grin.

Too many purple eyes glowed on her face.

The figure lunged at him, and he stumbled back a step as a young, panicked scream echoed in the space. The monster phased through him in a mist, but when Kennex whirled in place he witnessed a younger version of himself screaming and begging for her to stop. His mother swung her arm back to gain traction and Kennex reached out to catch her wrist. It was solid. Slowly, the figure turned to look directly at him as he tightened his grip. The mimic tilted its head in question, and he leaned in.

"Leave. *Now.*" The words were pushed out in a whisper. The weight they carried did not match the volume of his voice. It struggled against his hold for a second before disappearing in a wisp of smoke. His hand hung in the air where it had been.

"See? Was that so hard?" Lee teased from beside him.

Quickly, he grabbed her by the neck and dragged her up to her toes as her own hands clawed at his. Kennex took a slow breath through his nose. "You're not Lee. You're not the mimic. What are you?"

"A friend," it choked out. "I'm only visiting."

"Think of a better answer." He squeezed harder.

It tried to shake its head. "I only wanted to help. To show you the truth." It beat on his arm. "*Please.*"

Kennex let his fingers loosen. It fell from his hold and only barely managed to catch itself—hunched over and gasping for air. Finally, it stood back up, but it no longer resembled Lee. It was Ari.

Kennex ground his teeth as he stared at the discoloration around her throat. The bruises in the shape of his fingers. "You control the narrative, Kennex. Don't you see?"

"Stop." He stumbled back.

It matched his step, moving forward. "The power is in *your* hands. You get to decide. *You.*"

Kennex's mouth went dry. He tried to find a detail that wasn't right. Something to help him separate this figure from his Ari.

"I'll admit I was worried. She picked quite the guardian to stand for her, but you..." It chuckled. "You're probably the only person in the entire system that can stop her, and I am honored to have you in the light."

"What the hells?" Kennex's question faded as Ari's hand found the side of his face. It wasn't her. It wasn't her. He chanted the words in his head as a reminder, but it didn't help. Everything matched so perfectly. From the calluses on her palm to the smell of the soap she used. Every aspect of this reflection of his partner drowned him. He couldn't help but lean instinctively against her hand.

"This is where you belong," she murmured. "It's us against the worlds, Kennex."

- NINETEEN -

Travel via warp from Illyarium to Kharees took days. The worlds were relatively close neighbors as their orbits aligned, and it was, in part, why they were allies in trade. However, nine years ago this bond solidified further with the birth of the Expressway—a miracle of technology and science existing as a travel path between worlds. Located at the edge of Sector One's shipyard, the loading station housed three cruise liners that could carry passengers from Illyarium to Kharees via Expressway in two hours. Kennex could recall the broadcasts announcing its creation. It had been the buzz of the system—so much so that it reached even Acheron.

He found himself studying the cruise liners with reverence. They were works of art with black, glossy metal jutting out in sharp angles. Red accents traced the outer lines of each ship while neon colors in blue, green, pink, and purple hugged the internal designs. Alpha Ark, Iota Ark, and Rho Ark. Each one landing in the matching Quadrant of Upolent.

Another whispered murmur filled the air, and Kennex shifted uncomfortably as the pack of him, Vira, Brin, Lee, and Tryptan walked to the station. Coming out of the court had been a spectacle. Yarians stood outside the walls all hours of the day in hopes to see an Ascendant, and when the group of them stepped out the crowds had gone wild. Vira stated they were always there. Every day, regardless of the weather conditions. They stood, they waited, and they worshiped.

"Aether, look at them!" Tryptan beamed. Whereas all of them wore armor, the fledgling was dressed in normal clothes. He was out of the dark gray uniform and in something belonging on the streets. Specifically, the streets of Illyarium. The blazer, half bright blue and half white, with matching pants rolled at the ankles was not a style seen anywhere in Outer Orbit. He also wore golden cuffs around his ears that spread out like golden vines and leaves on the side of his head. "You know I've lived in Sector One my *whole* life, but I've never been this close to the station before. Which one are we going in?"

Vira was the one to answer. "Iota Ark." Her armor was bulkier than his with a tall collar around the back of her neck. The shape was slightly different than her mural, probably from upgrades, but the color remained. Burnt orange with accents of yellow and red. A navy cloak hung from her shoulders. "It's the closest to Epsilon. Only three quadrants away."

"I thought Alpha was three quadrants away and Iota was four?" Brin argued. His and Lee's armor matched. Brin's gear, clearly built for strength based on its thicker nature, was dark violet with light gray accents. Lee's was more slim with an inverted color scheme.

"And that's why we don't let you think," Lee teased.

"No, no, I'm pretty sure." Brin and Lee began to argue.

Kennex watched them from behind as their navy cloaks swished with each step. Brin's was thick cloth that hung off one shoulder while Lee's was see through with matching jewels embedded in it. He reached back to touch his own cloak. Black. Honestly, he felt comical wearing it. If even one person from his old life saw him in this, he'd willingly climb into a hole for centuries.

"You okay, new light?" Vira matched his pace. Despite the argument occurring up ahead, the five of them continued in the direction of Iota Ark. "You've been off since your last resurrection."

"I'm fine." Kennex shook his head. "I'm just—" He clenched his jaw and glanced around only to avert his eyes when he noticed the crowds gawking at them. "What if I don't like the answers I find?"

Vira hummed. "I don't know. Does it matter?"

"After all this, how could it not matter?"

"Because answers are answers." Vira shrugged. "Doesn't matter if you like or don't like them. Only matters what you do with them."

Kennex rolled her words around in his mind before looking to her. "There's another answer I want."

"Aether, *more?*"

"Why does Malachi trust you?" Kennex asked. Vira hissed for him to keep his voice down. He only lowered it a degree. "He obviously does because he put me with you. Then, he allows this." Kennex motioned to the station. "I want to know why. I can't trust you unless I know."

Vira sighed, "You almost hurt my feelings, new light." Kennex didn't respond. She glanced around and lowered her voice to near a whisper. "I told you. It's not trust, Kennex." He blinked at hearing his name in her voice. "It's a *stalemate.* He knows that he can't get rid of me. Can't just retire me. I'm a crowd favorite." Vira raised her arm in a wave and there was no better proof to her words as the crowd cheered and greeted her back. "But he also knows I can't just leave on my own. He knows I won't turn my back on the court or the people. So, this is the dance we're stuck in. We play our parts and wait for the other to make a mistake."

"What if neither of you make a mistake?" Kennex asked. He was coming to terms that not all Ascendants were how he imagined them. He had never expected an Ascendant to be like Vira. To care like she did. "How long can this go on?"

"Well, if there's one thing you learn as an Ascendant," Vira let out a dry chuckle, "it's patience."

Brin and Lee, settled in their argument, called for Vira and him to catch up. Tryptan continued to buzz beside them in visible excitement. Vira gave him a playful nudge with her elbow and hurried ahead. He readjusted his cloak again and followed.

Kennex was unsurprised when they were offered a cabin in first class rather than one of the seats on the lower decks. The cabin wasn't overly spacious, but it had six, large recliners. The tinted windows spanned the entire upper half of the wall allowing them a three-hundred-and-sixty-degree view. He could see other cabins on the top of the ark in matching bubble rooms.

"Wake me when we get there." Brin slumped into one of the chairs. Kennex was impressed at how fast he fell asleep.

Lee sat beside her brother flipping through the Otri journal. Vira reclined in the chair on the other side of Lee with her eyes closed. That left Kennex in the row across from them, and he frowned when Tryptan chose to sit next to him rather than a seat away.

"Have you ever been to Upolent before?" he asked.

"No," Kennex responded. Lee peered up from the pages of the journal to smirk at him and he blew out an exasperated sigh. Tryptan didn't note his discomfort and continued to ramble about how he also had never been. Kennex wasn't sure how the fledgling continued to find more to talk about.

"In fact," Tryptan shrugged, "I've never left Sector One at all. I've always wanted to, but it was expensive to leave the ring."

He had continued talking, but Kennex stayed hung up on a singular word. "Ring?" He interrupted. "I thought you said you'd never left Sector One?"

"I haven't. I'm from Sector One's overflow," Tryptan clarified. "My family and I lived on the ring. I came down for the Curator's Nest when I was eleven, and then a year later my family moved off the ring. They live downtown."

Kennex shook his head, still not understanding, "If you're from the Overflow Ring, how could you afford to go to the Curator's camp?"

"Scholarship." Tryptan shrugged. "I got chosen from my school as a possible candidate and they brought me to the Nest. Since I passed their tests, I got to attend full-time, and my family gets a stipend."

"Your family traded you to the camp for credits?"

"What? No!" Tryptan sounded aghast. "Of course not. This was like a perfect scenario. I always dreamed of being an Ascendant. Now, I get to train to be one, and they pay to take care of family so I can train guilt free. Without the stipend, I never would've stayed in the camp. My parents and my siblings needed me around to help provide." He grinned. "I got to help them in the *best* way possible. Living downtown? My mom has a *whole* garden to herself she can tend, and my dad opened a bakery he runs with my older brother, and my younger sister just got accepted to Sector Seven's University! They never would've had those opportunities if we had stayed on the ring."

Kennex sunk into his seat with a nod. "Oh. Sorry." He crossed his arms. "How, uh, when was the last time you saw them?"

"We have a visiting day once a year where we get to go home. Our last one was a few months back, but we do video calls all the time."

"Guess it's less of a prison than it looks," Kennex mumbled.

"I *love* it. Compared to the ring? It's a dream." Tryptan chuckled. "I know a guy who grew up in downtown Sector One, and he struggled in the beginning. But even he's gotten used to it."

"Yeah, well, you still have to deal with Kolche and that's a punishment nobody deserves," Kennex said. Tryptan laughed loudly, and he cracked a smile in response. He hadn't even meant it as a joke. After a beat, he cleared his throat, feeling more comfortable to speak to the fledgling. "That screwhead gave you the feathers for killing me, right?"

"Yeah." Tryptan grimaced. "Sorry again. I'm third in rank now though which is super great." Tryptan's eyes briefly widened as if he realized something and Kennex quirked an eyebrow at him. "Wait, this is your first official mission, right? Does that mean you're earning your wings?"

"Maybe," Vira cut in. Kennex glanced over to see she was peeking out of one eye with a grin. "Depends how much he annoys me on this mission."

"Okay, seriously," Kennex leaned onto his knees, "Earning my wings? What does that even mean? Ascendants don't have wings." He paused. "Do we?"

"Yes, we do," Lee added. She tapped at her left side, and it took Kennex a moment to realize her armor was engraved. A set of wings was carved into the metal over her ribcage. Lee followed it up by reaching over to grab Brin's collar. The sleeping Ascendant snored as his twin pointed out the wings engraved against the side of his collar.

"All Ascendants have that?" Kennex asked. His eyes slid back to Vira who lifted her arm. On the back of her right arm, just above her elbow, were a set of wings. "I didn't even notice them. Why is it so faint and—the location? Does that matter?"

"After an Ascendant's first mission, if they do well, they 'earn their wings' which makes them official. The location is a personal choice." Vira closed her eyes again and settled in her seat. "As for why they're hard to notice, they're for us only. The fancy, bright armor is for the crowds, but the wings? That's just ours."

Tryptan rambled about something else, pulling Lee into his conversation, but Kennex's attention stayed on the topic of wings.

***

UPOLENT WAS SO VAST THAT PARTS OF IT EXISTED IN SPACE. KENNEX wasn't sure what feat of engineering allowed them to build towering structures to live in the heat of the atmosphere, but it was a sight to behold. The angle of their approach allowed him to see a sliver of natural Kharees. From a distance the surface was dark red, and the edges of Upolent made the city of metal, glass, and technology look like a parasite. Branches of it clung to the surface as it were growing on the side of the word itself.

With its rate of growth, Upolent would cover the surface entirely in a few years.

Kennex was blown away as the ark drifted into the city. The engineering and technology he saw in Outer Orbit was a different kind of wonder. It was incredible what a person could produce as a solution when they had no real method of repair or replacement. Everything out there was just metal workings that existed far beyond their intended life. Creations for one task repurposed to another. Upolent was the exact opposite. Every glittering tower and ridge was polished and well cared for. There was constant movement as trains, lifts, and gliders cut their usual paths. The city had a thrum, a pulse, as if it were a living, breathing creature.

"We can take the warp rail to Epsilon," Vira said as they left the cabin.

"Warp rail?" Kennex questioned. "Like, real warp?"

"As opposed to the not real warp?" Lee joked. He shot her a dry look and she bumped her shoulder against his, the metal of their suits clanking. "Upolent is so big they use warp to move between the quadrants. Makes more sense when you're jumping more than two quadrants over."

Kennex shook his head. "But they're using warp capabilities on the surface of a planet? That's insane."

"Welcome to Upolent."

They stepped out the ark door to climb down a ramp, and Kennex couldn't keep his eyes focused on one singular thing. He wished he wasn't here with a specific goal and could just explore instead. In the distance was a building so long he couldn't see the end of either side. It just kept going.

"What is that?"

"The Academy," Lee answered. It needed no further name than that. The Academy was famous for the engineers it trained, but it housed schools of all kinds. Lee leaned toward him. "It's the size of Sector One."

Kennex was struggling to grasp the range and size of Upolent. Calling this place a city didn't do it justice. As they stepped onto solid ground, joining the masses leaving and coming toward the ark, he noticed a flicker of light above him just as a similar glow occurred above Vira, Brin, and Lee. Hovering over their heads were golden rings, like halos, and they stayed locked in place with every movement of their body.

"This is a joke, right?" Kennex deadpanned. He tried to swat away the halo.

"Told you Ascendants get marked," Vira replied. As they pushed further onto the station platform, Kennex also noted the reception was different. Crowds still watched them but now it was with hushed whispers and curious eyes. The handful of Yarians they passed would regard them with a bow of their heads, but the Khareesians' glowing bright eyes just followed silently.

Vira took lead, and as they reached a gate at the edge of the platform a Khareesian woman greeted them. She was dressed in the white gowns of a medical professional with vibrant red eyes. Her dark skin was adorned with golden freckles across the bridge of her nose and her pointed ears were cuffed with a gold ring on either side.

"Welcome to Iota Quadrant," She chirped in an accent that reminded him of Lain. "Please take note, Ascendants, that though you are truly welcome here with us you do not carry the authority you have on Illyarium. We ask you follow all laws and regulations in place."

"Of course," Vira responded for the group.

"Thank you. This is for the mortal Yarian." She pressed a latch on her belt and a small green pill fell into her palm. She offered it to Tryptan. "If you stay in Upolent for longer than twenty-four hours we ask you seek a medical professional to receive another dose."

Without asking for clarification, Tryptan tossed back the pill, and they were on the move again.

"What was that for?" Kennex asked.

"The air," Vira answered. "It'll protect his lungs and keep his blood clean."

"I thought Kharees had a similar atmosphere to Illyarium."

"It does. This is new," Vira continued. Kennex was pleased the group of them seemed as eager to answer his questions as he was to ask them. "The last couple years they've noticed the air in Upolent has been changing. It's something the tech gives off? I don't know. It's damaging to everyone though. Yarians and Khareesians."

Lee nodded. "I think they're working on solving that problem. I'm surprised they haven't already."

"Then shouldn't we have taken it?"

"Hey, new light." Brin pointed to his halo with a grin. "You'll heal faster than the damage can even collect."

"Oh. Right." Kennex mumbled and ran his hand through the halo mindlessly. The group moved on, seemingly unfazed by the sights around them, and he trailed after them.

- TWENTY -

Epsilon Quadrant matched the others in grandeur. The Academy had long ago faded from view, left behind in the warp, and now he was surrounded by plant life. This portion of Upolent was made up of mostly tall, spiraling towers, and on the side of many of the buildings were lush crops. As the group of them exited the airship onto a platform, Kennex slowly tilted his head to the side to examine the greenery.

"This is Turkina Farms," Tryptan announced in tour guide fashion. "Neat, huh? My mom told me Kharees used to be all farmlands. The world was, like, created to nurture growth." He shrugged casually. "That must have been a long, long time ago though."

Brin shook his head. "Kharees still has farmlands outside of Upolent." As if on cue, Kennex and Tryptan both glanced to Lee for confirmation. Brin scoffed, "Seriously? I know things too!"

"Brin is actually right about that." Lee chuckled. "They're not very popular though. I mean, why would you buy produce out there when you can get it sourced here in the city where it's genetically engineered to be perfect?"

"Hey, focus up," Vira called out. Attention shifted to where she stood at the edge of the platform. She nodded down. "The market is below us."

Kennex peered over the edge, and he couldn't make out where the towers even started. It all faded into a hazy, pink glow. "How far below us?"

"Very." Vira was scanning the air and when she found what she was searching for she lifted her fingers to let out a loud whistle followed by lifting her arm with a wave. A black airship broke from the traffic a few levels up and parked by the platform. The driver wore a helmet hiding any identifying features and the open craft was suited for a total of nine people. As they climbed in, Vira offered the pilot their location and the craft began to lower like a lift rather than move forward. "Alright, Tryptan, you know what we need?"

He nodded, hair bobbing with the movement. "Yeah! I find a Stellotrian and ask about, uh," he paused in thought then lifted a hand to read off his palm, "*See-ames* and *eunim*."

"Right," Vira said. "Meanwhile, we'll—"

"Wait, we're not going with him?" Kennex interrupted.

"New light, the whole point of bringing him was because no Stellotrian is going to talk while we're around." Vira leaned back in her seat. Natural light from Sol began to grow dim and was replaced with an artificial glow from the closest buildings. The soft pink and turquoise light surrounded them. "We have a mission to complete."

Kennex crossed his arms. "I'm not sending him alone." They only had one shot at this. He couldn't risk Tryptan failing. "He's the only one of us capable of dying." The fledgling shot him a broad smile that Kennex ignored. "Look, I'll go with him and keep a distance. Just watch from afar and make sure nothing goes wrong."

Vira had an argument caught behind her pressed lips. He was getting good at recognizing the very specific look of skepticism and mockery that filled her blue eyes. However, she turned to Lee, sharing a glance he did not understand, then back to him with a sigh. "Fine. You and Lee will accompany Tryptan. Brin and I will take care of the mission."

"Is this a good time to ask what the mission is?" Brin chimed up.

"There were a few active missions on Kharees, but the one I grabbed is target removal in Zone 23 of Epsilon Level Sub-186," Vira replied. Upolent was split into quadrants, but each quadrant was designated by levels and then further split by zones. The warp rail had left them on Level Zero of Epsilon, and Magus Market was on Level Sub-186. The mission was only a few zones away from it. Kennex's eyes widened, and she beat him to the punch. "Yeah. Convenient, huh? I'd be skeptical, but this mission has been active for thirty-three years."

"Why has it been active for so long? Is that normal for missions?"

The twins shook their head, and Vira kept a stoic face when she answered. "Because nobody wants to deal with a nether bust."

As the airship continued to sink, Kennex pondered over her words. Everyone knew nether's origin was Otradu. Pockets of trade existed all over the system, they had to for the drug to be so widespread, but finding them was no simple task. It made sense one of these trade spots would be in a Stellotrian community. What didn't make sense to Kennex was why no Ascendant would put an end to it.

Nether was poison, and it corrupted everything it touched.

They parked and it may as well have been a new world. Kennex stepped off, scanning the poorly lit, rusted platform. For a second, he felt like he was in one of Acheron's back hallways. Oddly, it made him miss Haven.

"If you keep on this path it'll take you to the market." Vira motioned ahead. "Brin and I are gonna find the target. Call us when you need us, Lee."

They slunk away before Kennex could question the mission further. Lee took the lead with Tryptan walking between them. He cleared his throat to snag her attention. "She never said who the target was."

"Would you like to forgo this badly planned audible of an already terrible plan and go with her?"

"This was your plan too. You agreed."

"Yes, but I never denied that it wasn't terrible."

"If you guys want to go with them," Tryptan's voice sounded nervous to chime in, "I can go alone. I promise. I won't mess this up for you, Kennex."

Kennex bit back a sigh and offered Tryptan a small smile of reassurance. The decision was made, and they were on the move. There was no backpedaling now. It was hesitation that got people killed on jobs. As they traveled, Kennex noticed that the dark was beginning to disperse. Sol's rays were reaching them and above it looked like the tall towers were growing shorter and more sparse. This trend continued until Kennex's eyes found land on the horizon rather than more metal workings and platforms.

They were on the edge of Upolent.

He drifted to where the platform abruptly ended. No railing offered safety to pedestrians. It just fell off into nothing. Kennex glanced down and several hundred stories below them the base of Upolent met the ground of Kharees. As seen from space, the world's dirt had a reddish tint. There was no vegetation or foliage anywhere. A few rivers existed of pitch-black water that traveled far off into the distance where a dark lake sat. It reminded him of Diomedes.

"It would be better if they just finished the expansion and covered the world," Lee murmured. She stood to his left and her eyes were on the skyline. "Right now, there's just needless suffering out there. The planet is *rotting*."

"Yeah," Kennex agreed, "I haven't seen many bodies of water in my lifetime, but that isn't nearly as welcoming as the pictures."

Lee shook her head. "That isn't a body of water, edger. That's oil runoff from Upolent." Kennex's eyes snapped back to sight. "My father has been on Upolent's board for decades. If they could just fully expand then the runoff could be shipped off world, he says. The rebels have kept them from being able to move forward."

She continued to walk with Tryptan by her side as if she hadn't just left him with more questions than answers. Kennex glanced at the black rivers once more before jogging after. They only had to walk a few minutes more before the silence between them was broken by the noise of civilization.

As they grew closer, the noise mingled with the smells of rich food and burning nether reminded him again of Acheron. They slowed before stepping into the view of the market. Kennex wanted to be near to ensure this plan worked, but he realized being in sight of the Stellotrians was really tempting fate for failure. He peeked around the corner to a wide alley filled with booths and plastic tarps. The crowd was a jumble of Stellotrians of all shades, but he could spot a few other races in the mix.

"Hey, I just saw a Yarian." Kennex pulled back. "I thought you said we weren't allowed in the Magus Market—"

"Shh!" Lee glared at him. "Don't call it that here. Even if they didn't hate you on sight, they certainly would if they heard you."

"I didn't say the full word, just magus."

"Right. Semantics will save you from their wrath."

"You didn't correct me before."

"We weren't surrounded by Stellotrians before, edger." Lee rolled her eyes. Kennex understood the word wasn't a kind phrase to refer to Stellotrians, but he wasn't foolish enough to call a Stellotrian "magusnaut" in conversation. "Tryptan, you have the credits I gave you?"

He patted his blazer pocket.

"Good. Find a Stellotrian working one of the booths. One that's not too busy and offer them the credits for an explanation as to how the words may be connected. Get whatever information you can."

Tryptan offered Kennex a bright grin. "Don't worry. I'll get you what you need."

He slipped around the corner without another word and Kennex slumped in annoyance. The fledgling seemed eager and capable, but Kennex hated leaving anything up to chance. Lee leaned against the wall with a shrug.

"Relax. He'll be fine." She jutted her chin toward the corner. "Plus, I attached a tracker and recorder to his clothes on Illyarium when he wasn't paying attention." Kennex raised an eyebrow. "What? I want to be able to listen to the conversation later."

Kennex couldn't find it in him to complain about the invasion of privacy. He didn't right care. With nothing but impatience to distract him, Kennex's mind drifted back to their earlier conversation. "So, your father is on the board right now?" Lee nodded. "He's not dead?"

"Of course he's not dead." Her eyes widened. "Brin and I visit him. Brin more than me. That's why it's even more embarrassing that my brother barely knows the quadrants."

"But you—How old are the two of you?"

Lee shot him a skeptical stare. "Do you not know?"

"It's not like we've talked about it, and usually when I ask you personal questions you dodge them," Kennex argued. "I know you're younger than Vira."

Lee crossed her arms and twisted her lips. Kennex waited, his eyes tracing the engraved wings on her suit's side. Finally, Lee nodded. "I ascended at twenty-five, like everyone else, but Brin and I have only been

Ascendants for seventy-eight years." Ninety. "Add that to the fact that my father is Khareesian. He turned 137 last year."

Lee was half Khareesian. It shouldn't have caught him off guard considering how vibrant her eyes were, but he assumed she was fully Yarian. Kennex thought all Ascendants were. The question must have been clear in his eyes because she let out a quiet, amused scoff. "Yes, we're half Khareesian, and it makes us *so special*." Her tone was mocking. "My father never shuts up about the studies he was able to conduct on my mother, and how his genes allow us to be a far superior breed of Ascendant."

"That's..." Kennex tried to find a word that wouldn't be insulting.

"Absurd? Pretentious? Delusional?" she offered. "Yeah, I know. It's why I hate visiting."

"I'm sorry." He knew a spoken apology didn't touch on the scars left from the trauma a parent left on their child. She acknowledged his words, but her eyes were cast down to her boots. "I never knew my father."

Lee's eyes glanced back up. "You were raised by your mother?"

"Raised is a strong word," Kennex chuckled. "She kept me fed and clothed until I was old enough to be the caretaker."

"How old was that?"

"Five? Six?" he shrugged. "I don't remember. To be honest, there's not a lot I remember before Ari." That's how his life could be separated. "Before Ari" and "With Ari". Every memory tied to her in some way as if she were the unit he used to keep measure of time. He hadn't considered much on "After Ari". Kennex didn't think a timeline like that would ever exist. "I met Ari right after my mom tried to kill me while high on nether. I was eleven."

"I'm sorry." Lee's voice was as soft as her lingering gaze. She seemed to understand how weak those words were in the grand scheme of things, but sometimes a sentiment was all one could muster up. Lee startled with no visible reason, but Kennex understood when her hand touched the communicator in her ear. She listened for a moment before nodding. "Tryptan's on his way back. He says he got it."

Kennex's first reaction was shock, but it melted into relief. One step closer. Lee flinched, a brief hiss slipping from her lips, and a tiny streak of shimmering gold appeared on her cheek. He narrowed his eyes and reached out to brush his gloved fingers against it. A drop of something cold landed on Kennex's head and his brow furrowed at the flash of pain that followed.

"What the hells?" he mumbled and rubbed at his head. A few more drops. "Rain?"

"*Scrap*. Acid rain," Lee pushed Kennex out of the way to rush into the alley. Kennex was tight on her heels, and they watched as booths and tarps were rolled up and packed away as the crowd scurried to safety. He spotted Tryptan as the masses thinned. The fledgling held his arms over his head as he ran toward them. "Tryptan!"

The raindrops were coming faster now, thunder rolled in the distance, and Kennex's scalp and face stung at each contact. Halfway to one another, Tryptan stumbled and hunched over as he dropped to a knee. Simultaneously, Kennex and Lee both picked up their paces. Lee reached the fledgling first and yanked him back up to his feet, so the boy wasn't kneeling in a puddle of acid. Kennex ripped off his cloak to throw over him.

"Lee!" Kennex barked.

"I know, I'm looking!" She shouted back as they scanned for safety. Lee was banging on doors, and the few she tried were locked. All the buildings were a part of the towers themselves and no awnings existed for them to duck under. The rain was falling steadily now, and it was beginning to eat through the thick material of his cloak. He heard Tryptan cry out in pain.

Kennex cursed and pushed Tryptan toward Lee who tried to also cover him with her arms. The building to their left had a door Lee already tried, but Kennex barreled toward it. His shoulder slammed into the metal, and it crumpled in the middle. Kennex reared back and hit it again. On the fourth blow, the metal snapped and fell to the floor causing him to stumble in. Lee didn't hesitate to shove past him, dragging Tryptan with her, and Kennex finally let out the breath of panic he had been holding.

"Tryptan." Lee yanked off the black cloak, letting it fall to the ground, and began to examine him. "Are you all right?"

"Yeah, I'll survive." Tryptan offered a grimace of a smile. Holes were scattered about his blazer, focused in on the shoulders and sleeves. Pink, tender skin scattered his arm in dots when Lee pulled up his sleeve and a few streaks of pink burns existed on his face as well. Kennex's eyes landed on the fledgling's knee where a bit of bright red blood began to soak into the burnt edges of his pant leg. "Thanks for getting to me."

Lee sighed, "Aether. What the hells was that? Upolent is supposed to be shielded from acid rainstorms!"

"Not this far out," a new voice chimed. Kennex stepped forward so Lee and Tryptan were behind him. An older woman sat behind a counter. Her skin was a pale blue. Wrinkles of age distorted the darker blue lines stained onto her features in sharp lines that fell from her hairline of snow white, braided hair. "The shields do not cover the edges of Upolent. You should count yourself lucky. This is just a cloud burst, not a deluge."

Kennex glanced down at the remains of the Stellotrian woman's door and huffed, "I wouldn't have knocked your door down if you had just opened for us when we knocked."

"Why should I have let you in?"

Lee pushed past him and motioned back to Tryptan. "We have a *mortal* with us. He could have—"

The woman held her hand up and shook her head. "Your reasons mean nothing to me. I do not care. Save your breath." Lee scoffed in disbelief, and the woman came around the counter. Her gait was slow, but she used a cane to keep steady. Kennex expected the clothes of this area to also resemble the worn-out look of most of Outer Orbit, but the woman was dressed nicely. The black dress was made of thick material and embroidered with purple swirls and flowers. What looked like a cream, hand knit shawl covered her shoulders. She whacked her cane against Kennex's leg, and he stepped out of her path in surprise at her gall.

She paused in front of Tryptan and narrowed her dark eyes at him. "Hmm, come, boy."

"Yes, ma'am," Tryptan replied.

Lee shifted closer to Kennex as they watched the boy follow the woman back toward the counter. She pulled out a chair and ordered him to sit before disappearing into a back room. Tryptan obeyed but squirmed in his seat.

"Do we trust this?" Lee didn't let her glare waver from where the Stellotrian had disappeared. Kennex glanced around the room and realized it looked like a small restaurant. Tables with the chairs turned up onto the surfaces filled the tiny space. "She's rude."

"Some would say that about you," Kennex said. Lee shot him a dry look and he chuckled. "Hey, you said the Stellotrians wouldn't like us. This isn't surprising. As soon as the rain stops, we'll leave."

"Still, I—" Lee stopped when a chirp came from her vambrace. She glanced down and tapped at the screen. "It's Vira."

Lee tapped the communicator in her ear to connect the call and drifted to a corner speaking quietly under her breath. Kennex turned his focus back on Tryptan who sat in the chair with his leg bouncing—his hands wringing together in his lap. Kennex crossed the room to question the fledgling about his findings, but the woman was back before he could utter a word.

"Foolish for bringing a mortal here," she scolded. "You heretics can make any deranged decision you want, but to subject a child to it—"

"I'm not a child," Tryptan pouted.

She shushed him and opened a tin of purple oil. The old woman dipped a finger into it and swirled the thick fluid around.

"Whoa, hey, what are you—" Kennex began to complain when the Stellotrian smeared the oil over one of the burns on Tryptan's face. The fledgling flinched, but it was short lived as relief crossed his features instead. "Huh." The woman searched him for burns and applied the oil to every spot she found. "What's your name?"

"Yonna."

"Well," Kennex cleared his throat. "Thank you, Yonna."

Tryptan echoed the sentiment with a warm smile. Kennex's eyes darted to Yonna's outstretched arm as she reached out to apply oil to a spot on Tryptan's shoulder through his burned clothes. Scars were scattered along her skin in a familiar pattern. There was one story of Ari's guardian that stuck with him in particular—one that touched on their culture. He only knew it because Kennex asked about a seemingly random scar on his partner's arm.

"What constellation is scarred on your arm?" Kennex asked. Ari had mentioned stars on her guardian's skin. A lifelong dedication of the Stellotrian to their favorite constellation in the sky—a method of worship or something like that.

Yonna knelt to where Tryptan's knee was burned and bloody. She adjusted her shawl to cover her arm then carefully began to rub oil onto the wound. "What do you know of the stars, heretic?"

Kennex stepped closer and realized all the other wounds she had smothered in oil were already half healed. He hesitated at the sight but shifted back on track. He grabbed her by the wrist and pulled the shawl back. Her dark eyes narrowed to glare up at him.

"Kennex," Tryptan whispered.

Unperturbed, Kennex pointed to her skin where the scars sat in a diamond formation. "*Eunim*. This constellation. It's *eunim*, isn't it?" Surprise filled her features and Kennex smirked. "I'm right."

Yonna tried to pull her arm away and Kennex released her on her second attempt. She stood with her tin of oil and stalked back to her counter. "To speak the name of an empyrean so arrogantly." She muttered in Otri. "You are all the same."

"Empyrean," Kennex repeated. "What is that?"

"*See-ames*!" Tryptan blurted, and if Yonna had looked shocked at Kennex's statement, she was doubly so at the boy speaking an Otri word. "That's what that means! The guy I paid said so. Gods and goddesses. He said *eunim* is a *see-ames*! Like Aether or Erebus."

Yonna began to speak in Otri as she moved her hands in a circular motion touching portions of her face and chest as she chanted the words. When she made eye contact again, she shook her head. "You know not of what you speak. They are not gods." Lee had ended the call and drifted over. "They are *energy*. Beings of energy bottled into a vessel to be used."

"You say they're not gods, yet your kind scars themselves in worship," Kennex replied.

"This." Yonna dragged a finger along the dots and lines of her scars. "This is *not* worship. This is remembrance. This is a blessing. This is the sky I was born under." Kennex wondered if he had misremembered the story Ari shared about her guardian's marks. "Eunim hung in the sky when I entered into this universe." She spoke a long string of words in Otri, and Tryptan cautiously rose from his chair to move toward Lee. Yonna snapped her arm out to point at Kennex. "My empyrean manipulates light, channels it, and learns from it." The Stellotrian was crossing around the counter now to approach him. "And the blessing gifted to me is one of knowledge."

In a blink, Yonna scratched his neck with a finger and tore skin. The pain was so fleeting that Kennex didn't even have time to register it. He watched the glow from his skin cast light on the woman's features—the silver stars in her dark eyes glimmered.

"Kennex Hall, you are *haunted.*" She stumbled back and muttered in Otri under her breath. Kennex called out to her, confused, but she skittered back behind her counter. "Leave me, devils."

Tryptan limped quickly to the exit and Lee followed. Kennex didn't move. He stared at Yonna who had resumed what looked like prayers. Lee murmured his name, tugged on his elbow, and he allowed her to drag him away. Outside, the rain was a light sprinkle. Tryptan had folded up Kennex's cloak and held it over his head best he could. All his wounds improved save for his knee.

"What was that about?" Lee whispered, glancing over her shoulder. "Did I miss something?"

Kennex shook his head. "What was she saying? Did you catch it?"

"Some of it." Lee frowned, clearly displeased that her question had been avoided. "She was begging for protection, I think. I'm not sure though, she was speaking too fast and quiet."

He should have known better. Often, finding answers just led to more questions. Knowledge was an endless venture. It was why Kennex found enjoyment in it, but right now the pleasure of solving a puzzle was missing and only confusion remained. As it sat in his gut, turning sour as the seconds passed, it evaporated into anger. And, in the billowing smoke of his rage, Kennex was blind. He couldn't understand how Ari survived like this—it was suffocating.

"Look, we can puzzle all this out on our way home." Lee set her hand on his shoulder. "Vira says she needs us. They got pinned."

- TWENTY-ONE -

O n one of their first jobs as task runners, Kennex and Ari got pinned in the burnt-out husk of a small house for two days. They had been sent to shake down a man that owed Recluse credits, but the man had more friends than him and Ari had bargained for. It was through sheer determination they kept the men back and pure luck that the men were too stupid to just bomb them out. Eventually, Recluse showed up and saved the day in his typical fashion. He slaughtered the men and then beat the scrap out of Kennex and Ari for needing his help in the first place.

Kennex didn't understand how Ascendants could get "pinned down" as Lee claimed.

He and Ari had been trapped because if they slipped up the men were going to "rip out their entrails and make 'em eat it." The nonsensical threat had a permanent place in his mind. Occasionally, Ari would quote it as a joke between them.

This shouldn't have been a concern for Vira or Brin though.

Lee, Tryptan, and Kennex followed instructions to a warehouse and, upon finding it, their first sight was of Vira and Brin crouched behind a fallen, metal pillar. Beyond them, the warehouse was a shoddy, metal structure built onto the platform they were located on with no connection to the neighboring towers. Vira barked out at them just as a few stray plasma bolts fired. Kennex grabbed Tryptan by the back of his neck and shoved him down. Heat splashed up from the opposite side of the pillar as the yellow bolts made contact.

"You okay?" Vira asked. Her eyes zoned in on Tryptan's knee. The fledgling nodded breathlessly. "All right, we—"

"What are you two doing?" Kennex hissed.

Brin and Vira shared a glance before Brin snorted. "Knitting, new light. What's it look like?"

Kennex glared in response to the jest and the Ascendant blinked at him in confusion. He could barely fault Brin's response. A voice whispering at the back of his mind was telling Kennex he'd eventually feel bad for responding to Brin in this way. However, regret came later.

"How could you get pinned? Just walk in there and take care of it."

"It's not that simple," Vira said.

"What isn't? Who is this target?"

"His name is Oracle Kamori." This information was new to Lee, Tryptan, and him, but Vira's gaze was firmly locked on Kennex alone. He met her intensity with a glare. "He's a Stellotrian in the nether business. That's his base of operations. We need to take him alive."

Kennex shook his head. "Okay? Where's the complicated part? We go in and grab the bastard."

"Did you miss the part about that warehouse being a base of operations for the nether business?" Brin asked with a lack of his usual amusement. He had shifted to sit on the ground with his back against the pillar casually. He thumbed the air behind him. "We start a firefight in there and it'll blow. Nether in liquid form is more flammable than starship oil."

Kennex glanced over the top of the pillar to the warehouse. Though he had been confused at how Ari could function with anger seemingly always in her veins, Kennex began to experience clarity. Staring at the warehouse, he craved a fight.

What would Ari 'Lucky Fox' Barlow do?

Reckless decision made in response to the question, Kennex leapt over the pillar. He heard voices yell his name, felt Vira's grip briefly on his arm, but he was already running.

Yellow plasma bolts began to rain down again, but Kennex didn't keep his path to the warehouse a straight one. Plasma worked in degrees. Red was the cheapest—slow and prone to overheating. Blue was the most expensive and by far the best—crisp energy and quick cool down periods. Various colors sat in between that spectrum at different prices and skill. Kennex used to use green which was medium in every category. Yellow sat only a step above red. It was why he reached the front doors of the warehouse without a scorch mark on him.

Bursting in, the closest attacker was a Stellotrian who turned to fire. Kennex slammed his fist into the man's chest and felt bone shatter under his gloved hand. The man went sprawling back into two others. Another rushed to tackle him, and he lowered his shoulder to catch the man and flip him over. Kennex's boot came down to crush the wrist holding an energy blade. He spun to rush forward, and bright yellow heat caught him in the face.

Kennex blinked.

He was in Joon. A wispy memory of Ari stood in front of him dressed in her gear. She activated her helmet and the glowing orange lines of a fox sigil appeared. He did not stay. Kennex closed his eyes and found himself in midfall as the sounds of a firefight engulfed him.

Kennex hit the floor and rolled over his shoulder back to his feet. Lunging forward, he caught the man who had killed him by the throat, a Rikilian, and threw him into a stack of barrels that exploded in a plume of nether.

"*Kennex*!" Vira bellowed behind him, but he didn't slow.

He did not seek out enemies, but he mowed down the attackers that approached him on his path. A Stellotrian tried to stab him with a metal blade, and it shattered the second it contacted his suit. He grabbed the Stellotrian's hand, holding the broken blade, and twisted the arm to bury the sharp hilt into the attacker's chest. Seconds after, heat exploded on the left side of his face.

Back in Joon.

Ari was limping with her arm stretched out to where he should be. With only her flight suit on, the left arm mauled to ribbons, she was pale and breathless. Drops of blood fell to the stone and red moss sprouted where they landed.

Kennex blinked.

Falling again.

He caught himself by his hands before he could hit the floor and pushed up just as quick. He yanked the broken hilt from the chest of Stellotrian beside him and whipped around to throw it. Kennex wasn't nearly as accurate as Ari with his throws, but it clipped the Yarian with a hand cannon on the side of the head and sent him to the floor. He heard Vira again, but he had reached the back of the room where a broad set of stairs took him up to the second floor.

A metal sword swung out at him, and he ducked the blow. Somebody from behind wrapped their arms around him. Kennex kicked his head back, felt the crunch of a nose breaking, and turned to shove the Stellotrian down the stairs. When he turned back around, the Yarian with the sword swung again and the dull blade buried into the side of his neck. He choked. Breath lost in his injured throat. But, he didn't hesitate. Kennex grasped the sword and pulled it deeper.

Two blinks and he was back in Joon.

Ari was on her hands and knees in front of him. Wounds patched sloppily with foam as she tried to catch her breath without collapsing.

"Wait," she gasped in a hoarse voice.

Kennex hesitated. He wondered what would have happened if he hadn't left Recluse's shuttle to try and disable X'ael's ship. Maybe he should have closed the hatch, raced up to the flight deck, and tried to escape. That wasn't what happened though.

Ari's shaky hand tried to grab his leg, but he had already taken a step away. *"Kennex."*

Kennex came to, knelt on one knee, and he looked up to see the Yarian with a sword staring at him. With a grunt, Kennex slammed his fist into the man's knee. It bent back at the wrong angle and the Yarian fell with a scream. A janky hand cannon was tucked into the man's waistband.

He grabbed the flailing man by the collar, snatched the hand cannon, and threw him backwards down the stairs. Rising to stand, Kennex found only one other soul in the room filled to the brim with cargo. The Stellotrian was rapidly typing at a holodesk. He was dressed sloppily in a short sleeve jacket over a dirty white shirt and pants. A crown of sorts wrapped around the back of his head, nestled in his black hair, and branched up in front of his ears to match the curled red lines on his pink face.

At Kennex's approach, Oracle Kamori tried to sprint to a door at the other side of the room. For the first time since Diomedes, Kennex pulled a trigger. The yellow bolt hit its target. Not the man, but the barrel by the door. It exploded and threw Kamori back. Kennex stalked toward the Stellotrian as the purple flames began to eat away at the rest of the room.

"What have you done!?" Kamori shouted. He tried to scramble away, but Kennex buried the end of the hand cannon onto his chest while crouched beside him. The Stellotrian hissed as run off plasma oozed from the poorly cared for weapon and singed through to his skin. "You just destroyed it all!"

"Good," Kenned replied. "Nether has no place here. Should've kept it on your own fraking planet."

"My planet?" Kamori laughed. "I'm *from* Kharees. I was born here. I'm a citizen, you devil." Kennex noticed the pink skin of both arms were marred with the open wounds of a junkie, but no well-placed scars of a constellation. "And just you wait until everyone finds out a fraking Ascendant attacked and killed a bunch of Stellotrians."

Kennex tapped the hand cannon against Kamori's chest making him hiss in pain. "You think I'm here because of the color of your skin? The blood in your veins? I don't care about any of that. I'm here because sons of whores like you ruin lives with this fraking drug."

"I don't ruin *scrap*," Kamori spat. "You think I push nether into their veins? Make them drink it or snort it? *No.*" The temperature of the room was sweltering, and the metal structure groaned at the stress of it. "I didn't create the demand; I just make credits off the supply. It's called good business, devil." Kennex locked his jaw and a smug smile spread across Kamori's features. "Let me guess. Someone you love died of a nether overdose because they were too stupid to keep track of what they were putting in their body, and now you have a penchant for putting *monsters* like me in our place. Is that why you became an Ascendant? Serve justice?"

Kennex's finger twitched on the trigger.

A hand clamped down at the back of his collar and threw him back. Kennex grunted as he slid across the floor.

"What the *frak* do you think you're doing!?" Vira roared over the flames. Kamori was chanting his thanks as Kennex glared at him. If he had his hand cannon, the one he tailored and adjusted to his preference, the twitch would have ended the Oracle. Vira snapped to Kamori, "*Shut the hells up!*"

She grabbed him by the shoulder and dragged the Stellotrian to the nearest window, "Whoa, whoa, you just *saved* me! Why kill me now?"

"The fall won't kill you," Vira replied before throwing him out. Kamori's scream was lost in the noise of the fire filling the room. Kennex stood and coughed as noxious smoke filled his lungs. Vira rounded on him. "You *stupid* bastard."

"I did what had to be done!" Kennex yelled back. "What *you* should've done!"

"Who gets to decide what has to be done or not?" Vira stormed to him and grabbed him by the front of his suit. Kennex dropped the hand cannon to grasp onto her hands. "You? A new light that's existed in this universe for twenty-three years!?" Vira shook him hard. "I don't give a damn what Malachi says. You are *not* that special, Kennex!"

Vira shoved him back. Kennex held her heavy glare until the smoke in the room grew almost too thick to make out her figure. She shook her head and stalked to the same window she had thrown Kamori out of. Kennex watched as she jumped and left him in the flames.

Purple heat crackled and closed in on him, but Kennex felt cold.

The cold was numbing, and it crept over every inch of his soul like a forming frost. Kennex was beginning to associate the sensation with loneliness. When Ari had come into his life, she filled the gaping hole in his chest. She was like Sol. An overpowering, radiant, blinding light filling him with warmth. Now that she was missing from him, the hole was back, and it was engulfing.

Kennex wanted to stay in the flames. He prayed the heat would eat away at his skin, muscle, and bone—warm his soul. Even if it did, it wouldn't last. Kennex would wake up again with this same hole in his chest, and the sinking feeling that he was losing himself to it.

- TWENTY-TWO -

The others stood away from the inferno that was once a warehouse. Oracle Kamori sat on the ground by Brin's feet in cuffs. Tryptan had Kennex's cloak wrapped round his neck and shoulders. It had been pinned to create a makeshift mask to cover the fledgling's mouth and nose. As Kennex approached them, he was aware that patches of hair at the back of his head were missing and most of the skin on his face and neck were shimmering from fresh burns.

"I already contacted emergency services. They're sending fire management," Lee spoke to Vira, but her eyes drifted to meet his. She turned to him. "Kennex—"

"Go," Vira commanded. "Take Kamori to legal services, and then head back to the court. Kennex and I will follow later."

Kennex's eyebrows rose at the words. Brin nodded without hesitation and scooped Kamori up to toss over his shoulder. Lee shot him another glance, worry evident in the violet gaze he was growing accustomed to, as she led Tryptan away. With a sigh, Kennex glanced over his shoulder at the growing fire. The warehouse had collapsed in on itself and after a loud groan it sunk through the platform floor. Flames remained, too far from the towers to touch them, but they stretched to reach the closest other structures—almost like an starving animal clawing to a meal.

"Vira, I don't want—"

"We're waiting here for fire management, then we have errands to run."

Kennex didn't have the energy, or stupidity, to press further on the topic of errands. They stood in silence, watching the fire grow with no ability to stop it. Though it felt like a lifetime, only a few minutes passed when fire management arrived at the scene. The fire team arrived via multiple airships. Some hovered near the fire using turrets shooting water to try and control it. One landed as a few Khareesians rushed toward them. Vira met them halfway and Kennex could faintly hear her explaining the situation.

They thanked her and rushed to action. Vira returned to him, but she walked past without a word. The Ascendant made no motion or sound for him to follow, but with a muted sigh he did.

It wasn't until they were on a airship rising back to Level Zero of Epsilon that she finally spoke. Vira stood from her seat while the ship was still moving, "Deactivate your suit."

He watched as she tapped on her vambrace. Brightly colored metal folded back into a pauldron. Vira shot him a glare and he rose to do the same. It wasn't as if removing their suits made it any easier to blend in. Even if they were able to hide the glowing halos above their heads, the clothes they wore stood out as distinctly Yarian—distinctly Ascendant. They both wore uniforms. A white skintight, short sleeve shirt with a half neck tucked into a set of pants with multiple pockets that he found handy. On the left side of the shirt, over the heart, the Ascendant sigil was stitched in. Obnoxious in appearance, but Kennex did note that it fit under his suit comfortably.

"Where are we going?" Kennex asked, sitting back down.

"Epsilon has a shopping district," Vira responded plainly.

Kennex stared at her, unblinking, and waited for further information. She simply looked down at her vambrace and typed. He sunk in his seat and stared at the scenery that had shifted back into the brightly lit and clean atmosphere Upolent was known for. When the airship reached the main platform, it didn't stop. It rose further and joined the flowing traffic of other airships. In the distance, Kennex spotted a large, multi-story rectangular building that was nestled between four towers. Growing greenery and glass made up the walls.

The airship parked on a platform under the building and Kennex followed Vira off.

"Look, if you're gonna scold me, can we just get to it?" He huffed while following her—ignoring the curious glances of those they passed. Vira led him toward a lift but rather than taking it up into the building, she took the stairs beside it that led to a platform just below the one they were on. Small cafes and restaurants sat on this platform with a medium sized crowd. Vira veered off to one where a Khareesian cooked a noodle dish right in front of those sitting at the bar. "What is this?"

Vira sat down and patted the seat beside her. Kennex hesitated, confused, and she had ordered dishes by the time he finally sat. She cleared her throat and pushed her orange glasses to rest atop her head. "You'll heal faster if you eat. You burned through a lot of energy on your warpath."

Kennex didn't bother lying about not being hungry. At the savory smell of food being made, his stomach was trying to eat itself. He waited for Vira to speak again, but she patiently sat beside him until he couldn't stand it anymore.

"Do you want me to apologize?" he asked.

"Lee mentioned you have a bad history with nether," Vira interrupted, and he stiffened. "She didn't give me specifics. She was just trying to explain to me why you did what you did." Vira chuckled. "She was trying to protect you which is honestly funny considering the two of you met with her blade bursting through your chest."

Kennex rubbed the back of his neck. "I don't have a bad history with nether. I never touched the scrap. My mom did. I have a bad history with *her*." Vira hummed in response. Kennex laced his fingers together in front of him and his knuckles lightened at the tension there. "I hope it isn't an apology you're looking for because I'm not sorry." Again, Vira only hummed. He gritted his teeth before hissing out. "It had to be done."

"Why?" Vira asked.

"Because it—" Kennex forced himself to take a deep breath. "How many lives are gonna be saved with that nether trade site down? Without

Oracle Kamori pushing it, how many people did we prevent from becoming addicts one day? What happened was—"

"Was for the greater good?" Vira finished. Kennex nodded. "What's your math on that, new light? How many lives does it take to meet that criterion? One? Ten? Does it just have to outweigh the lives lost?"

Kennex laughed. "Lives lost? You mean the junkies that tried to kill me?"

"I don't think it counts as attempted murder if you're incapable of death."

He ignored her and jabbed a finger into the table to emphasize his words. "They hardly count, is my point. They threw away their lives when they started using nether."

"Hmm," Vira leaned against the table, "I thought someone from Outer Orbit would be more lenient on someone addicted to nether." Kennex narrowed his eyes at the insinuation. "I mean, drugs are just a coping mechanism. A cover."

"They don't get to use life being difficult as their excuse." Kennex turned in his seat to face her. "Ari and I had a *scrap* life. More went wrong than right, but we *never* touched the stuff. We made it through without it."

Vira didn't shift her body toward him, but she did turn her head to face him. "Right. You two never got addicted to nether. You just became bloodthirsty task runners for a criminal. If only everyone was as *well-adjusted* as the two of you."

Kennex lost his breath as if a punch had landed up into his diaphragm. The suffocating sensation reminiscent of being surrounded by billowing, nether smoke. He ground his teeth together. Kennex hissed, "You don't know what the frak you're talking about."

"Actually, you'd be surprised how much I know." Vira paused when their food was delivered. She focused on the bowl, stirring her noodles in the broth, but Kennex couldn't bring himself to look at his own meal. "I looked into this Recluse guy. Did some research on Lucky Fox and Venom. Seemed like you two kept busy."

"What kind of research are you talking about?"

"I have a few sources through the system." Vira shrugged and took a bite of her food. She tapped the table by his bowl, and he sighed before stirring his own meal. The savory scent of the dish had gotten hard to ignore.

"Whatever information you got from the enforcers or acolytes out there—"

"Didn't get it from them," Vira interrupted. "Why would you assume my sources were enforcers and acolytes?" Kennex had a bite of noodles halfway to his mouth when he paused to look at her. She had an eyebrow raised in question, but he didn't offer a response. "Most of my sources are hunters. One mercenary whose ego makes getting info from her painful, and a few ordinary denizens of the Meridian System."

Kennex scoffed, "Why would they help you with anything?"

"Because we're *friends*." Vira chuckled. Kennex let the bite of food fall back into the broth. She shook her head. "Aether, help us. I didn't think that would be a foreign concept." Vira let her utensil rest against the rim of her bowl. "From the jobs I've heard about, the people who have had run-ins with you... You've been in survival mode for a while. The reputation I hear is that you were the guard dog. Nobody ever dealt with just Lucky Fox alone. They had to go head-to-head with her shadow as well." Kennex huffed and turned to his food, finally managing a bite. "To me, it sounds like you're not new to being a protector. And Ari Barlow—"

"Watch it, Vira," Kennex warned, his voice guttural and tense.

She paused. "Why did you assume I was going to say something negative about her?" He glanced over. Vira's eyebrows were furrowed, but Kennex struggled to differentiate if she were confused or curious. Kennex locked his jaw. "I think Ari Barlow is a fighter, and I mean that in the *best* way possible. I have never, nor will I ever, look down my nose at strength just because it comes from a different part of the system than the one I know."

Kennex felt his shoulders slump in relief. Ari *was* a fighter. She was the strongest woman he had ever met, and it was nice to hear it acknowledged from someone else. He rested his arms on the table and sighed.

"Vira," he mumbled, "Why are you bringing this up? I don't—I don't understand what point you're trying to make."

"You are not Venom anymore," Vira replied.

Kennex closed his eyes and rubbed at his face, still half slumped onto the table.

"I know that isn't something you want to hear, but it's true and I think you know it's true."

Venom had died on Diomedes. A concept that filled Kennex with palpable fear. He did not feel like Recluse's task runner anymore—hadn't for quite some time now. Nothing in this universe could alter his perception of Ari, but Kennex was terrified that when they reunited, she wouldn't recognize him. "You don't like being called an Ascendant, I get it, but you can't deny the responsibility now in your hands."

Kennex finally reopened his eyes. "I never asked for this responsibility."

"Neither did I," Vira admitted. He slowly leaned back in his chair, keeping his gaze on her. She shrugged. "Nobody's talked to you about my Ascension yet?"

"No."

"I was already half dead when I ascended," Vira admitted. "When I was twenty-seven, Drucanna and Illyarium were at war." Kennex's eyes widened. He didn't know this. "War is maybe too big a word. Drucanna just liked to attack from time to time. They used to be bold enough to do things like that, but they've since calmed. It cost thousands of live though." She hummed. "Sector Three of the Overflow Ring got hit in an attack. Nearly everyone from that portion of the ring died, and the devastation rained down on Illyarium. That's where I was living with my family while training to be an enforcer."

Kennex wasn't sure what he was more surprised by, but the question chose itself. "Your family?"

"I was married. We had a kid." A small smile pulled at Vira's lips. "That morning we had been planning for his fourth birthday. Jena was making a cake. She couldn't bake for scrap, but she was trying." Vira chuckled but the silence that followed was an echoing agony. "Long story short, I lost everything in the span of sixteen seconds. And, when the legionaries—Dracck soldiers—came to the surface to continue the attack, I...I blacked out. I don't remember the rampage I went on, but they told me I killed seven legionaries. That I—I had one of their blades sticking straight through me as I fought.

"Ascendants arrived. For some reason, Malachi was with them that day—I do remember that. I had come to just in time to see him kneeling over me with that weird, fraking dagger, and I remember him burying it into my chest." Vira shrugged. "I woke up an Ascendant."

"Vira, I... I don't know what to say." Kennex mumbled. The only sound came from the crowd around them going about their day. He finally shook his head. "What was his name? Your kid?"

Vira smiled. "Reise." She pointed toward him with her utensil. "This might sound weird, but you remind me of him sometimes." Kennex's eyes widened in surprise, and he was again at a loss for words. "He was too curious for his own good, too."

Kennex hated how often he thought or claimed Vira to not know how he felt. If anything, she was the only person in the system who understood what it was to lose an entire life and awake in a new one. An apology got caught in his throat.

Vira rolled her shoulders, stretching her neck, and coughed. "The point I'm making here, new light, is I understand the temptation of revenge. After earning my wings, I went on any mission involving legionaries. I went beyond mission parameters. I wasn't just protecting; I was serving my own brand of justice. The system was a better place without those bloodthirsty, Dracck soldiers in my mind."

"But were you wrong?" Kennex muttered. "They killed innocents."

"It wasn't my place to decide that. Not me alone. That's not justice," Vira replied. "Being Ascendant doesn't make us special. It doesn't make us smarter or kinder or better than anybody else. It doesn't give us the right to decide who lives and who dies. It just gives us the responsibility to protect those who can't fight for themselves."

Kennex was desperate to prove his point. "But that's what I did. That's what *you* did. The legionaries you killed, Oracle Kamori and his junkies— they were *not* innocent."

"Sure, but our actions have consequences, Kennex. If you blindly use your newfound Ascendant status to even a score, then somebody is going to have to pay the cost. And as an immortal, that cost is *never* going to fall on your shoulders." Vira said firmly. "On one of my rampages, I killed a kid." Kennex stiffened. "He was no older than you. He was scared. Ran out while I was fighting, and I was so blind in my hate that my weapon buried in his chest before I even realized who he was. Do you know why Brin and Lee weren't in the warehouse with me chasing after you?" The question was so out of place it took Kennex a second to even recognize it. He shook his head. "I sent them to the platform under the warehouse. There's a neighborhood on that level."

Nausea overwhelmed him.

"Don't worry," Vira said. "Luckily, it was a smaller neighborhood, and the twins evacuated the houses in time."

"*Aether*." Kennex breathed and buried his face into his hands as he slumped against the counter. He was in shock at how stupid, how reckless, he had been. Kennex was better than that. He prided himself on thinking through his actions. Rash decisions were Ari's calling card, not his.

"There are some out there who see mortal life as second tier. They'll be gone one day regardless of what we do. But, I think their lives matter more because of how fleeting it is. The passage of time is a gift that no longer belongs to us." Vira nodded. "What else are we here for if not to preserve life and allow them the time they're blessed with?"

Vira motioned to his bowl and ushered him to eat. He ate his cold noodles on autopilot. Kennex always told Ari they could be better than what Recluse built them to be. This was his chance to prove that true. Vira seemed to believe in him. Enough so to take the time and teach him this hard learned lesson.

Only a few bites of his meal remained when he asked, "Are there actual errands to run or was that an excuse to get me alone?"

"Oh, no. I have errands." Vira bobbed her head and the orange glasses slid from the top of her head to fall in place. "Lyris' birthday is coming up soon. I need to get her a gift."

"That's nice." Kennex hummed. "The two of you are good friends, huh?"

Vira snorted a laugh and nearly choked on the broth she was drinking from the bowl. Kennex narrowed his eyes as she rubbed away fallen drops from her chin. "Yeah, new light, we're *really* good friends."

It took two beats for him to catch her insinuation and his eyes widened. Kennex glanced around as if they were sharing a secret. "But she—she's *married*. To a man." Vira nodded with a gloating smirk. "Are you sure she's—I mean, how do you know she's..."

"How do I know that she likes women as well as men?" Vira asked for him. Kennex gave a weak shrug. "Good question. You know what? Next time I'm eating her out, I'll ask."

Kennex covered his eyes with his hand as his cheeks burned. If he willed it hard enough, perhaps the universe would spare him, and a hole would open beneath him to swallow him whole. It had been kind enough to bring him back to life that first time, after all. Perhaps it was also kind enough to offer a mercy kill. Vira was laughing and Kennex shook his head. "Frak. I'm sorry. Can you just kill me?"

"No, I think I like watching you suffer."

Kennex sighed. "This might also be a stupid question, but if the two of you are involved then why is she still married?"

"It is a stupid question, but you're new to Illyarium so I'll let it slide," Vira replied. She pulled some credits from her pocket to set on the counter then motioned for him to follow. "She married the piece of scrap as an adherent by an acolyte *'in the eyes of Aether.'* Separation is only by death. Nothing else." It sounded like a flawed and dangerous system of marriage, but Kennex couldn't have expected much more from Aether's Light if he thought about it. "Plus, even if she could leave him, relations between mortals and immortals is frowned upon."

"But Lee and Brin's parents—"

"Frowned upon, but not strictly enforced," Vira emphasized. "Besides, their father had status—something to offer. Malachi was more than happy to let it slide since it strengthened his relationship with Kharees." She nudged him. "I don't know Ari's lineage, but if she miraculously has a parent with political power or millions of credits then the two of you should be fine."

Kennex shook his head. "Ari and I aren't involved like that."

"Sure, new light." Vira rolled her eyes. "Come on. Quicker we find what I'm looking for, the sooner we get back home."

- TWENTY-THREE -

The gift Vira chose ended up being a silver bracelet. It was one of the simplest pieces they found, but she had deemed it perfect. Kennex had his legs kicked up to take up the seat beside him as it was only him and Vira in the ark's cabin this time. His goal had been to sleep, but when it didn't find him, he chose to stare out the window.

"Oh, I never asked," Vira called out. Kennex turned his head to see she was sitting like him. She had been asleep the last hour so she must have just woken. "How did your information seeking go? Did the kid figure it out?"

Kennex nodded, but sighed, "Sort of. He got answers, but everything I learned just—"

"Created more questions?"

"Yeah."

Vira chuckled. "Color me surprised."

"This Stellotrian woman we met helped out."

"A Stellotrian helped you?"

"Eh," Kennex wavered. He explained the cloud burst of acid rain and how they ended up in the woman's restaurant against her will. "So now we know Eunim is a god—or empyrean—like Aether, but I still don't know why Malachi thought I needed to know that or what it has to do with the kid he tried to sacrifice."

Vira groaned. "I hate relying on Malachi for anything, but he makes a habit of forcing your hand. If you come to him with this 'empyrean' information, then maybe he'll give you the next word for you to look up. Knowing him that's his plan." She scoffed, "Pretentious bastard."

Kennex ran through the information he knew about empyreans in his head, in preparation to bring to Malachi, and it was as he planned that the dots finally connected. He straightened in his seat, spinning his legs around to plant his feet on the ground, and sucked in a sharp breath.

Vira called out his name, but he stayed silent.

All he had learned circled back to Yonna's words.

Beings of energy.

VIRA DIDN'T SEEM TO TAKE IT PERSONAL WHEN KENNEX RACED OFF the ark. He didn't linger on the streets of Sector One to be gawked at. In fact, he ran back to the Court of Aether. His pace didn't falter until the tower's lift was in sight, and even then it was only because a voice called out to him.

"Lee," he greeted without stopping. "Hey, I—"

"What happened?" She was out of her armor, the pauldron gone as well, and back into casual clothes. Worry was worn on her features. "Did you and Vira work it out?"

Kennex nodded. "Yes. It's fine, but I have to go."

"Actually, we need to talk about something." Lee grabbed his elbow. "It's about the Magus Market."

He hesitated, steps faltering, but he shook his head. Kennex set a hand on top of hers and offered a tight smile. "I—I gotta see Malachi. *Right now.*" Lee's eyes widened. "But, I'll meet you back at my dorm, yeah?"

"Sure." She nodded. "Is everything okay, Kennex?"

Kennex squeezed her hand but offered no reply. He could feel her eyes on him as he resumed his pace, and when he stepped into the lift his last sight before the doors closed was Lee watching.

Staring at himself in the lift's glass was familiar. Not much time had passed since he was last here, but his reflection revealed how much had changed. Kennex set his hand over his chest and a part of him expected the movement in the glass to not match. But, it did. This was him.

As the lift neared the top, Kennex reached under his collar and hooked his thumb under the gold chain. He pulled until the charm could be seen.

Kennex had full plans to barrel out of the lift to Malachi's office, but when the doors slid open, he froze. Sol's fading rays couldn't reach the top of the tower, leaving the hall surrounding the garden dark. Red robed acolytes, tenders to the garden, stood on the stone facing out as if on guard. He could only see them because of the lights emitting from the garden itself. White orbs, in various sizes, floated in the air, and the plant life glowed. On autopilot, he drifted into the garden and the grass under him lit up where his boots made contact—leaving a trail of blue footprints.

Despite the humidity, Kennex's skin pebbled. His palms were clammy, and anxiety was vibrating up every nerve fiber to his spine. Physically, he was on edge and wary, but there was a soothing peace that suffocated his mind in a thick fog. Ducking under a dark branch with glowing veins of bioluminescence weaved though, he found the source of water creating the light tinkling in the air. A small waterfall pooled into a pond where even the plants at the sandy bottom stretched up to the surface with the same glow as everything else. It tinted the water a light pink.

Standing in front of the pond, facing away from him, was Malachi. The crisp white suit was clearly his, but what gave Kennex pause was the head of thick, wavy silver hair. He wasn't wearing his helmet. Though his mind offered the realization, it took a second to fully click. Kennex's jaw fell open, but all his words jammed in his throat.

"Welcome home, Kennex," Malachi greeted. "I assume your trip went well?"

The religious leader turned and Kennex stumbled back a step. Under the medium length, silver hair was pale pink skin. Malachi's features were gaunt, cheeks hollow, and the shape of his almond eyes curved down at the ends. A starry gaze stared back at Kennex as he traced the deep red lines on Malachi's face. Two lines traveled down from his hairline to form a point on his forehead. Two other lines, starting in the same location but falling straight down over his eyes, went all the way to his chin and neck where it then disappeared into the collar of his shirt.

"You're Stellotrian?" Kennex gasped.

"I am in this lifetime."

The shock had thrown him, but Malachi's response brought him back to focus. Kennex stormed forward until he was an arm's length away from the man. He pointed at him. "Eunim." His teeth grit. "*You're* Eunim." A tight-lipped smile graced the Stellotrian's features. Kennex growled out his next question. "How?"

"What makes you so sure?"

"Aether, Erebus, Eunim—They're *see-ames*. Empyreans," Kennex repeated the newest word added to his vocabulary. "Beings of energy that are bottled into a vessel." He jabbed his finger into Malachi's chest. "That's what a Stellotrian woman told me. The constellation on her arm was of Eunim, and she said he was a—a being that manipulated, channeled, light. That he learns from it. She was blessed by him, or whatever, but she nicked me." Kennex grabbed two handfuls of Malachi's suit to jostle him. "Just like you did when we met. That's how you knew so much about me, you bastard. Have you been in my head this entire time?"

Malachi tsked, "No, Kennex. Many of my siblings have gifts born in the light, but entering a mind is not something I am capable of. I have not been in your head. That is not my gift. I can simply, as she so aptly put, *learn from the light*." He carefully grasped Kennex's wrists and ripped his hands off his jacket. In response, Kennex jerked out of his hold. "It's how I know all my Ascendants. I am not insincere in my care for them—every Ascendant is a part of me. I do not take that facilely."

Kennex took a step back. "It's you." Malachi tilted his head. "Aether has nothing to do with Ascendants. It's *all* you."

"Yes, but I do so in Aether's name. It is his will," Malachi argued. He clasped his hands in front of him, bobbing his head, while that star-filled gaze stared right through Kennex. Malachi peeled a finger up to point at him. "*Your* will."

Kennex shook his head, repeated the words in his mind. "Wait, what?"

Malachi lunged forward and Kennex was too stunned to react. Pink hands grabbed him by the shoulders, eyes wild with excitement, as he grinned. "Aether. You are Aether." Kennex tried to shake loose, but the Curator's hold was too tight. "I do not understand what could have happened during this lifetime to have trapped you in this vessel with no control, but you are here and that is what matters."

"You're out of your fraking mind." It wasn't a question.

"For some reason, this vessel's soul is still so present." Malachi finally released him. He paced away while rubbing his jaw and neck. "I thought surely the more you learned, the more you resurrected, it would diminish Kennex Hall."

Kennex grasped Ari's charm as if it were a lifeline. "You aren't—"

"We do not die. We cannot die." Malachi quit his pacing to stalk to him again and Kennex tried to backpedal. "We are simply reborn again and again. Typically, we wake in our new vessels when the vessel goes through puberty or a significant time of fear, but you didn't appear until Diomedes. Was it meeting Erebus' vessel?"

"Erebus' vessel?" Kennex questioned.

"Perhaps, just the act of dying itself—"

"Wait!" Kennex took another large step away from Malachi and his boot stepped into the shallow pond. He was gasping for air as his chest tightened and ached. The sky was crushing him and his new location in the pond placed him a foot shorter than Malachi who now towered over him. "You said Erebus' vessel."

Malachi nodded. "The child." Kennex shouldn't have been shocked that it all went back to the child hiding in the tree on Diomedes. "I have been preventing Erebus' return for far longer than anyone could know. And for the first time, I failed you. I am so sorry."

The girl was Erebus reincarnated. Kennex struggled to remember her name.

"I suppose I technically knew this day would come. It was prophesized," Malachi sighed. "Ohni is a nuisance, but she is rarely wrong in her visions." Kennex furrowed his brow at the unfamiliar name. "But now, we can resolve this. *Together.*"

"Why—" Kennex's voice was hoarse from how dry his mouth had become. "Why are you telling me this now?"

"I had hoped learning on your own would spark your full emergence—"

"Stop talking to me as if I'm—"

"But, clearly, I was wrong," Malachi finished. "This is my new attempt. Perhaps a resurrection once you know the full truth will be enough."

The word "resurrection" had only barely left Kennex's lips in question when Malachi tackled him into the water. Kennex's head went under, and his heart leapt to his throat. He scrambled and fought with Malachi's arms. Briefly, he was able to lift his head enough to gasp for air, but it was short lived. Kennex went under again and the back of his head hit the sandy bottom. Malachi's boot found it's home on his neck.

Spots danced in Kennex's vision as a vague, distorted image of Malachi peered down at him from above the surface. He clawed at Malachi's leg, but it didn't budge. His heart pounded in his ears, his lungs ached, and Kennex's last breath failed him. Instinctively, his body gasped for air but only found fire. Water surrounded him, buried him, but it was a burning inferno that ripped through his throat and filled his lungs. The spots grew larger until he could see nothing, but the fire remained.

- TWENTY-FOUR -

The sensation of falling was short lived as he jerked and startled awake.

Warm hands settled on his shoulders in comfort.

"Whoa, hey," Ari chuckled, "You're okay."

She had spun on her stool to face him. The sounds of the Barrel surrounded him: a group of hunters playing Seven Suns in the corner, Trig berating a customer down the bar for spilling their drink, the mechanical hum of Acheron's machinery. Kennex fell at ease. He relaxed in her hold. Ari smiled, and he realized it wasn't right. There was no hint of too many teeth or skin pulled too taut. In fact, the crooked grin carried the same playful energy she carried with him. Everything about it looked normal, but it just wasn't right.

It wasn't Ari.

"You're not her," he mumbled in agony. Kennex realized it was foolish of him to think it could be. That this could have all been some nightmare his brain concocted after falling asleep at the bar. He turned his head to look at the shelves of liquor and in the reflective backdrop of those shelves he saw an Ascendant staring back at him.

Kennex shrugged out of her hold. Ari let her hands drop to her lap. "Sorry. I thought this form would bring you comfort." It did. That's why he hated it so much. "I know this isn't the life you thought you'd have but—"

"Am I Aether?" Kennex asked.

Malachi made it sound like this resurrection would wipe his identity away. Kennex didn't know if that meant he wouldn't wake up. He wasn't in Joon anymore. Perhaps that was a bad sign. Though, if his afterlife was sitting at the bar with Ari for eternity, he must have done something right during his lifetime.

"No," she responded. "You're not Aether." The Ari lookalike turned to face forward as he did, and she set her hands on the bar. Kennex met her gaze in the reflection in front of them. "I am."

Kennex's mouth went dry as he followed Malachi's earlier words. "If you're in my head, am I your—"

"Vessel? No, no," they shook their head. "I didn't mean to startle you with my presence. I can visit the mind of any living being." Kennex furrowed his brow and Aether chuckled. "It isn't like that. I can visit, influence and speak, but my presence is a passive one. You are still in control. I knew this would be the easiest way to speak to you."

"Malachi—Er, Eunim. He thinks I'm you."

"Yes, well, Eunim is a very loyal ally, but he can be..." Aether rolled their hand in the air searching for a thought, but they ended it with a shrug. "Let's just say, there is a reason I have not revealed myself to him yet." Kennex didn't have an argument or anything to add. He had spoken to Malachi enough times to understand the sentiment. "In a perfect universe, I would have no need for him, but the nature of his gift allows me an ally through time."

Kennex narrowed his eyes. "Because he's Ascendant?"

"That's the name he made up for it, but yes. Immortal." Aether nodded. "Only three empyreans have no need for resurrection. Only three can withstand the test of time, due to the nature of their gifts, and he's the only one I can trust." Another statement that left him with more questions than answers. Aether bobbed their head. "But, he is not a fool. He is right about the child."

"The one we found on Diomedes."

"Yes." Aether nodded and turned in their seat. Kennex mimicked their action, but it was unsettling to speak to a supposed god while staring at a copy of Ari. "Erebus' vessel escaped Diomedes thanks to your partner. She slumbers now, but when she wakes, we will all be in danger."

If Kennex were being honest, the "we" Aether spoke of was a secondary concern. One stood out. One always stood out. "Ari," he said. "Ari is in danger being with Erebus' vessel?"

"Not quite," Aether wavered. "Not how you believe, at least. I want to be honest with you, Kennex, so I will not hide information for the sake of your emotions. Ari is not in danger of being killed by Erebus because she was already killed by Ascendant X'ael." Kennex could physically feel his heart stop. It froze along with the breath in his lungs and the blood in his veins. Aether held their hands out placatingly. "But so were you! You both perished on Diomedes, Kennex, and you were both brought back."

Kennex sucked in a gasping breath, and he was forced to turn in his seat so he could settle his nerves. He rubbed his face with one hand while the other gripped the edge of the bar. When he finally caught enough air to speak, Kennex let his hand fall from his face. "Are you saying she's Ascendant too?"

"No. The energy that brought you back was very different than hers," Aether replied. "I'm quite familiar with the creature that brought you back. I've had several brushes with them in the past thanks to my gift." Aether motioned across the bar to where Trig served drinks. Her form was constantly shifting now. Skin color, hair, eyes, limbs, teeth, clothes. The mimic was not holding one form but rather moved in a constant flux of them all. "A creator. They weave the threads of life into a being."

Kennex never would have guessed a creature involved with life and creation could be so eerie and unsettling. He forced his gaze away and it instead settled on a spot of the bar top. Though he didn't understand the full degree of this scenario, he took comfort that Ari could be safe from death. Even if it were in a different way. With that comfort came the haunting echo of the Ascendants' warning. There are fates worse than death.

"Ari is still in danger though." Kennex lifted his eyes to the shadow of his partner. "What will happen to her if Erebus wakes up in her vessel?"

"I have never known Erebus to be merciful." Aether sighed. "She will destroy life, just to spite me, and when she finishes there, Ari Barlow's existence will either be wiped from the universe or she will be enslaved—forever tethered to Erebus."

"Forever? Erebus is like Eunim?"

Aether nodded—solemn. "Yes. She is one of the three, but she's the worst of them. Erebus does not require a reincarnation if she does not want it, and if allowed to gain her full strength she is the only empyrean who can exist outside of a vessel. The only way we've been able to force a reincarnation was through ceremony. Eunim, in his current vessel, has managed to keep Erebus contained for the 3,892 years he has been alive—using magik to bind her to Diomedes and destroying her with her own blade."

"The knife," Kennex mumbled with a nod. "There was a dagger stabbed in the tree."

"Yes. Exactly." They grinned. "Kennex, I know this is not the fate you wanted for yourself, but you have been chosen for a greater purpose. You can save everyone." The word "chosen" reminded him of a previous moment in this world between life and death. "Erebus will not stand a chance if we—"

"Last time, in my head," Kennex thought aloud, "you were here. You were Lee and then you were Ari, and you said she picked..." His eyes snapped to meet Aether's. "What brought Ari back? If a—a creator brought me back, then what brought her back!?"

Aether held their hands up with a sigh. "A reaper. An agent of death in the same sense of a creator being an agent of life."

Kennex felt his throat thicken in worry. The creator haunting him could only be described as a nightmare. A chill formed in his blood at the thought of what a reaper could have been to her.

"What—"

"You want to save Ari. Protect her." Aether emphasized. He nodded. "That will not be simple. We can do it—I know we can stop Erebus, but... Ari won't be saved easily. That reaper will have whispered lies in her ears and she will fight back."

Kennex rose from the stool so abruptly that it clattered on the ground.

All sound, all motion, in the Barrel froze. "I am *not* fighting Ari." Aether opened their mouth, and it infuriated him that they still used Ari's face. "I am not fighting her! Do you get that?"

"Then don't fight her." Aether shrugged with a laugh. They had spun to lean back against the bar with their legs crossed. They shook their head. "That's the beauty of you being chosen, Kennex. I said it before, you are the *only* being in this entire universe that might be able to convince Ari of the truth." They clasped their hands together with a sigh. "I know what it is to lose a partner. Erebus and I... If I could alter the path we ended up on, I would. I would give anything to return to what we were, but—" Ari's voice cracked as they spoke, and the sound made his chest ache. "I want you to save everyone, Ari included, and I pray that you can do what I didn't. I pray that you can show Ari the truth."

Determination slammed into him. He would. He would show her. Ari was smart. Clever and quick like a fox. But more so, deep down, Ari was *good*. If she knew the truth of what that kid was then she would see reason. Stubborn or not, Kennex would do what he failed to do all those years working for Recluse—what he failed to do on Diomedes.

He would convince her to listen to him.

- TWENTY-FIVE -

Kennex woke with Malachi crouched over him.

He took a deep breath, relishing in the way air filled his lungs, while glaring at the Stellotrian peering down at him. Malachi must have dragged him from the pond into grass. He used his talon ring to nick at Kennex's cheek. Gold reflected in the starry gaze studying him. Malachi's face contorted in what Kennex would label confusion. Going back to his roots on Acheron, the smell of the Barrel still in his nostrils, Kennex tucked his thumb between his fingers and twisted in the Curator's direction.

Malachi spat a curse and stalked away. Kennex ran his hands through his hair to push the damp locks off his forehead. His wet clothes clung to him uncomfortably, and when he pushed to stand, he left a puddle forming in the grass beneath him.

"I told you I wasn't Aether," Kennex snarled.

"You are just confused. I can—"

"Aether spoke to me." At the words, Malachi spun in place, staring at him with wide eyes. Kennex chuckled, smug, "Yeah. What's wrong? You can't see that when you read my light, you bastard? Shame. I'd like to see you hear Aether admit how he's avoiding you."

"You lie," Malachi hissed and stormed toward him.

Kennex didn't let the Curator's approach make him falter. He stood tall and tilted his head with a shrug. "But I'm not. Aether visited." He pointed to his head with a chuckle. "Told me the plan you're apparently not privy to. How sad is that? You've existed in this form for 3,892 years just for Aether to decide you weren't worth trusting."

Malachi stumbled back a step with a gasp. Kennex took pleasure in the pain that filled the empyrean's eyes. He couldn't physically hurt the man, but this form of attack seemed to work. Kennex closed the space and grasped Malachi by his jacket lapels.

"Fate didn't choose you. It chose two mortals from Acheron—two mortals who have been told our entire lives that we aren't worth scrap." Kennex shook him. "We died on Diomedes, were trusted with the immortality you hand out to further your own desires in the name of Aether, and now we're gonna use it to stop Erebus. We don't need you." Kennex shoved Malachi back and the Stellotrian tripped over his own feet and fell on his ass. He scoffed, "Aether doesn't need you."

Kennex took a second to memorize the agony drawn on Malachi's features then stalked out of the garden. He only got a few steps away when his name was called. With a sigh, he glanced over his shoulder. Malachi had risen from the ground and his helmet was hiding him again. Golden glass stared back at Kennex.

"If Aether has chosen you, I will concede that honor. But, if you believe Arienna Barlow has his blessing, you are wrong." Kennex stiffened and Malachi's haunting chuckle echoed around the garden. "She is *tainted*. She is poison to Aether's grand purpose. Heed this warning, Kennex Hall," Malachi spat his name. "This does not end with you by her side."

Kennex ground his teeth together as the words weighed on him. He held his chin high, and his confidence returned. "We'll see about that."

***

KENNEX FELT LIGHT. FOR THE FIRST TIME SINCE HE ENTERED THE COURT, he understood his path. This was what he had wanted from the beginning. Clarity. Answers. With those things came a calm. Kennex no longer had to attempt decisions from his gut, he could leave that talent to Ari, and he could make a logical choice. Saving Ari meant stopping Erebus, and he could do that. They could do that. There wasn't a job in the Meridian System that Ari and he couldn't take on together.

As he reached his dorm, Kennex was unhooking his pauldron from around his chest as the doors slid open and Lee's voice greeted him. She stood in the living room, as if having just risen from the couch, and stared at him in concern. Her hair was pulled up into a high ponytail and she had traded her usual clothes for something cozy. Thick, pajama shorts and a sweater he recognized as one she had stolen from his closet weeks ago.

"Why are you wet?" she asked as he drifted further in.

Kennex dropped his pauldron with a heavy thunk then ripped his shirt off to join it with a gross splat. "Uh," he pushed his damp hair back again, "Malachi drowned me."

"He what?" Lee hurried over but rushed past him. Kennex blinked in confusion until she returned from his room with a towel. "Why?"

Kennex took it from her and began to dry his hair first. "He thought I was Aether." Lee's jaw fell open as she blankly stared at him. "Yeah. Remember that Stellotrian woman said *see-ames*, or empyreans, were beings of energy in a vessel?" Kennex reached out to tap her chin and she closed her mouth with a nod. "Eunim is an empyrean and Malachi is the vessel he reincarnated into. He thought I was a vessel Aether reincarnated into—just late. He thought that explained Diomedes."

Lee crossed her arms. She opened her mouth only to close it then shake her head. "Well, are you?" Kennex shot her a light glare and she shrugged. "What? It seems worth asking. You would know if you were, right?"

"I know I'm not because I spoke to Aether, and he told me I wasn't."

Silence ensued as Lee blinked at him. She folded her hands together and pressed it against her face with a deep sigh. "Kennex, if you don't *fraking explain*—"

"Every time I die, I go somewhere. Kind of like a dream." Kennex let the towel hang around his neck. "Diomedes, but a Diomedes of the past. Sometimes I'd see my memories there, playing in front of me, but other times there are these creatures."

Lee had her fingertips pressed against her lips, one arm crossed over her chest, and she interrupted, "And one of these *creatures* told you that you weren't Aether."

"One of those creatures turned out to *be* Aether," Kennex replied. Lee pressed her lips together, and he chuckled. Kennex grasped her by the shoulders and nodded. "I know how this sounds, Lee, but listen."

Kennex walked through all of it. Every detail he had hidden to himself. Before, Kennex kept Joon a secret because it was his. Beyond the charm around his neck, it was all he had of Ari. Those small moments of reprieve were a gift and he refused to share that with anyone. Kennex found admitting this to Lee wasn't as difficult as he thought it would be. She listened intently as he rolled from the topic of his dreams and Aether right into the threat of Erebus looming on the horizon.

"Right." Lee's hand rested on the side of her face as she took in the information. "Is that everything?"

"Yeah—wait, no." Kennex shook his head. "Malachi is a Stellotrian." Lee's eyes widened as her hand fell to her side and he chuckled. "How bad is it that I almost forgot to mention that detail?"

"Well, there were plenty of other outrageous and ridiculous details to smother it."

"You believe me?"

"Of course," Lee replied without hesitation. "I'm just trying to figure out what this means for us. Where do we go from here?"

Kennex shrugged and grasped the ends of the towel around his neck. "Where we were always going. We find Ari, I explain to her what's going on, and we stop Erebus."

"You say that like it's all so simple, Kennex."

"It's not simple, but it's clear," he said. "This entire time we've had a vague plan of 'find answers' but now, we know, and we can plan accordingly. I know what happened to Ari and I... I know what I have to do—what *we* have to do. I've always worked best with a concrete plan in place."

Lee crossed her arms and blew out a breath. "Fine. It's all insane, but you're right. At least we finally have the answers. That is comforting."

"Thank you," Kennex blurted. Lee raised an eyebrow. "I owe Vira and

Brin a thanks as well, but I wouldn't have gotten these answers without you. Thank you for translating for me and spending your time here helping me." Her arms fell to her side. Lee's fingers tugged at the hem of the sweater swallowing her. "You, uh, you said there was something to talk about."

"It doesn't seem nearly as important now that you have all the answers," Lee mumbled. Her violet eyes met his, and in a beat of silence, Kennex noted how close they stood. Enough so that his chin tilted down to meet her gaze. "Have you told the others yet?"

Kennex shook his head. "Not yet. I need to. We can go find them now."

"Or we can wait until the morning," Lee replied. "V is probably with Lyris, and pulling Brin away from Rakerby's now wouldn't be worth it."

"I still haven't been there," Kennex murmured softly.

"It's a bar, Kennex," Lee said. "I'm sure you get the gist."

Every movement was slow. Kennex hadn't realized they were drifting together until Lee mumbled his name and her lips brushed against his. Even then, the merging of where he ended and she started was gradual—like an eclipse. The feather light brush of her fingers against his neck had his eyes fluttering closed. In darkness, Kennex felt so much more aware of the shape of her lips slotted to his. The taste of her took his focus. The familiar stirrings of arousal were sharply interrupted by guilt.

It soured his thoughts. Kennex pulled back with a gasp.

"Wait." He shook his head, trying to clear the distraction from his mind. "Lee, we shouldn't."

"Why?" she murmured. Her nails carded through the short hair at the back of his head.

Kennex tried to hold her gaze, but the intensity was overwhelming. "It isn't fair to you."

Of all the reactions he expected, he did not anticipate a broad grin. A breathless chuckle left her, and she shook her head. "Are you fraking kidding?" Lee continued to grin as she pressed the pad of her thumb to his lower lip. "Edger, I'm not in love with you, and you're not in love with me. This isn't about fair. It's about celebrating."

Needing no further encouragement or reassurance, Kennex knocked away the hand touching his lips to pull her into him. This time their touch was not slow. They collided in a tangle of flesh and desperation. Lee's teeth buried into his lower lip as his hands held onto her with a bruising grip—a battle of who could devour who faster. The fuse had been lit, a spark ignited, and the fire consuming him ran hotter than nether flames.

Breathless, Kennex slapped her thigh, already hiked up his hip, "*Jump.*"

He felt Lee grin against his lips as she did just as he said. Kennex caught her, hands squeezing the skin he held more for his pleasure than her support. Fingers combed through the hair atop his head and pulled enough to tilt his head back. She peppered open mouth kisses along the length of his neck as he carried her into the next room.

<hr>

Lee was soft.

As she laid her head on his chest, his fingers drawing invisible patterns up and down her spine, it was the thought that stayed with him. Kennex assumed as a warrior she would be as marred as him, but the only scar on her body was the Ascension mark between her breasts.

"How do you not have a mark on you?" Kennex murmured.

"What?" Lee turned from cheek to chin to meet his gaze. "Like a tattoo? Ascendants can't keep tattoos."

"No, I meant—what?"

"Yeah. If you had them before the Ascension then sure, but if you got a tattoo right now," Lee traced her fingers against his ribs, "then it'd disappear. Your body would heal."

The logic was there and Kennex chuckled that it hadn't occurred to him. "Right, no, I meant scars." Lee opened her mouth, and he tapped his fingers against her back. "Other than the one from your Ascension."

She smirked and grasped the hand not on her. Kennex allowed her to pull it toward the back of her head. Lee used her fingers to help guide his until he found a raised scar, about two inches long, hiding in her hair.

"When I was a kid, I fell down a flight of stairs and cracked my head open." Lee explained. "Also broke my arm, but that didn't leave a scar."

"How'd that happen?"

"I was being a brat." Lee traced the raking scars across his ribcage. "Trying to get my father's attention. I was tugging on his sleeve and when he jerked his arm away, I lost balance and tumbled back."

Kennex furrowed his brow at this. "What?"

"It's okay." Lee shrugged slightly. "He bought me the telescope I wanted after it happened."

"That doesn't make it okay," he scoffed. Lee only gave him another half-hearted shrug. Kennex raised an eyebrow at her. "Do you want me to kill him for you?" She let out a laugh and buried her face into his chest. His lips quirked up. "I'm serious. I'll do it."

Lee shook her head, "Oh, shut up, edger." A comfortable silence passed between them before her hand drifted down to brush against his abdomen. Kennex sucked in a sharp breath. "This is where your mother got you?"

"Yeah." He softly grasped her hand and pulled it up to rest on his chest. "Can I ask you something else, Lee?" She nodded best she could with her chin against him. Kennex hesitated. "Do you still love him?"

Lee's eyes widened for only a second before she steeled her features. She cleared her throat and turned her head to rest her cheek back on him instead. "Who?" Kennex mumbled her name and she sighed. "Of course not. It's been nearly a decade since X'ael and I have even really talked beyond a few passing words." Her voice grew softer. "It'd be pathetic of me to still love him. Wouldn't it?"

Kennex swallowed the lump in his throat. "No." There was nothing pathetic about housing love for any length of time. "Not at all."

"What about you?" Lee still didn't meet his gaze. "It must be hard to work with her considering your feelings."

"Working with Ari is the easiest thing in the worlds." Kennex shook his head. "Besides, she doesn't know." He felt Lee stiffen in his grasp. She pushed off his chest to turn and face him. Kennex sat up. "I've never told Ari I love her."

"Why not?" Lee furrowed her brows, and Kennex reached out to smooth out the lines with his thumb. "Kennex, why haven't you told her?"

Kennex let his hand fall away, and he sighed. "Because she's not ready to love me—to love anyone." Lee opened her mouth, and he shook his head. "You don't know Ari like I do. She's been through so much, and she's still working through it all. Telling Ari how I feel...I didn't want to pressure her."

"Would it really be pressure? She deserves to know."

"I know. You're not wrong, but Ari has a bad habit of giving too much," he replied. Kennex considered admitting the truth to her on several occasions, but it never felt right. "Earning her trust is hard. She rarely gives it out. But, if you manage it, Ari is the most loyal person in this system. She'd give you *anything*." Kennex knew sharing his thoughts, sharing his heart, would have pressured her into returning it, and he did not want her love as a reflection of his own. "Ari didn't need a lover; she needed a friend. A partner. Someone to trust, and that's who I am. That's who I will always be—whatever she needs."

Lee set her hand on his cheek, and he leaned into the comfort. "I get it now. You're just disgustingly kind and sacrificial." Kennex chuckled. "You know, I always assumed you and her would end up like X'ael and I. Now, I kind of hope we end up like Ari and you." She leaned forward to ghost her lips against his. "You're gonna find her, Kennex, I can feel it, and that kind of makes me hope that one day I'll find X'ael again. He's in there. I know it. Buried under everything Malachi has ingrained in him."

"You will." Kennex gave a small nod. He cleared his throat. "Last question, and this one might be the toughest so bear with me." He took in a deep breath and Lee brushed her thumb against his cheekbone. "How in the hells are you attracted to those creepy red eyes?"

"For Aether's sake," Lee groaned and rolled her eyes. She dropped her hand. "You're so stupid, edger. I'm leaving." She twisted to get out of bed and Kennex wrapped his arms around her waist to pull her back. He buried his lips into the crook of her shoulder, and she laughed. "Nuh uh, you're done."

"I'm nowhere near done with you," he argued.

Lee twisted in his arms to find his lips with her own, and Kennex let himself revel in the touch.

- TWENTY-SIX -

Rakerby's was not a regular bar.

For one, it was in a tree.

At the edge of Haven, right at the wall separating it from Sector One, was an old and gnarled tree. It didn't look like the tall, straight ones that filled the forests. This tree, though quite large, was wide with thick branches, twisted and curled into the air, covered in dark green and yellow leaves. Housed at the center, half hidden by foliage, was Rakerby's.

It was supposedly named after one of the Yarian builders who constructed the wall surrounding the court. This ancient tree, which fell directly where they wanted to build, somehow lived through the carnage of construction. It was supposed to be destroyed like half the hill was for the placement of the twenty-some story wall, but Rakerby argued on its behalf. They left the tree in place.

Now it sat on the edge, half leaning over air. Its roots grew over the thick stone wall and down—as if the poor thing was still searching for soil to bury itself in. Despite the changes, the tree lived on, thrived, and Rakerby celebrated its survival by building a bar among its branches.

Kennex read the story from a plaque resting on the bar top where he stood waiting for drinks. All of Rakerby's was shaped like a circle and at the center was the thick branch it was built around. The tree cut through the bar creating a towering pillar. The bar itself sat around the branch where three adherents tended to Ascendants. Shelves were drilled into the branch and held liquors, wines, and brews from all over the system.

He hadn't spotted any from Acheron to his dismay.

The rest of the room spanned out from the branch and consisted of various tables and booths for drinkers to reside in. The ceiling was tented in shape and string lights decorated the beams holding it up.

"What's taking you so long?"

At Lee's voice, Kennex glanced over his shoulder to see her stride to him. She took the barstool to his right, carefully adjusting her long skirt, and laced her fingers together on the counter.

"We're sobering up over there."

The raucous laughter and jests booming from a portion of Rakerby's behind him was a clear indicator that his slowness with the drinks was not interrupting the party held in Vira's honor. Her centennial. Today marked the 100th anniversary of her Ascension, and though Kennex had been enjoying himself up until now, he found himself mellowed the longer he was separated from them.

"He's working on it." Kennex nodded to the adherent making the drinks.

Lee spun in place and Kennex couldn't help but allow his eyes to trace the curve of her thighs, showing through the slits on her skirt. She adjusted the lapels of the suit jacket he wore then let her hand linger against his chest. "What's bothering you?"

"Nothing." Kennex shook his head. Lee shot him a skeptical look. He chuckled and turned his head to look at the shelves of alcohol again. The metal holding the bottles was reflective and he studied the view of him and Lee sitting side by side at the bar. "I'm just..."

Unable to find his words, he stayed silent. Lee let him stew for a moment before she tapped against the bar to gain the adherent's attention. "Deliver those to Ascendant Vira." She added a thanks when the adherent confirmed her order. Kennex mumbled her name in question, but Lee only grasped him by the hand and dragged him away from the bar. "Come on."

"We're supposed to be celebrating Vira," Kennex said when he realized she was dragging him to the outdoor patio.

"Vira is going to leave in a few minutes to be with Lyris. She won't even notice us slipping away," Lee replied. They stepped out onto the patio through a glass door, and when it closed behind them the sounds of the party muted.

Kennex let out a sigh of relief and walked to the railing. The patio was a half-circle on the backside of Rakerby's that opened toward Sector One. With the distance from this patio to the edge of the wall top, it was about a thirty-foot fall to the city. They stood among a gap in the branches, and it allowed Kennex a view of the glowing buildings. His lips twitched up in a small smile at the thought of how much Ari would like this spot.

Lee hummed. It drew his attention back to her soft features. "You're missing her right now."

"I always miss her," Kennex admitted.

"Yeah, but you feel guilt. You miss her, but you're here enjoying yourself with us."

Kennex crossed his arms on the railing and hung his head. "It isn't fair. I shouldn't be at a party. I should be back at my dorm trying to track her down—or in a starship searching for her."

After the entire fireteam knew what he did, they had decided to find Ari on their own. It had become a race between them and Malachi. Kennex needed to find his partner first. It was imperative. In order to convince Ari to trust his new Ascendant friends, to trust Aether, he had to be the one to explain the situation to her first. If Malachi got the first word in, a difficult mission could become impossible.

"Hey," Lee cupped his jawline and lifted his gaze back up. "You're allowed to take time for yourself, Kennex." She tapped her fingers against his cheek with a small smile. "From what I've gathered about Ari Barlow, she's plenty capable of taking care of herself in the meantime. And if she cares about you as you care about her, she'd want you to rest. Take a break and have fun every now and again."

Kennex grasped the hand against his face and held it. "Am I getting that easy to read?"

"No. Unfortunately for me, we're just very alike," Lee replied.

He wanted to ask more about X'ael. The creepy Ascendant was an enigma, but there must have been some redeeming fate deep down for a person like Lee to care for him. As tempted as he was, Kennex held back his curiosity. Instead, he focused on the way her hand felt against his skin. Kennex missed touch. He had never admitted to Ari how he craved it. She wouldn't have understood, and he didn't fault her for that.

Another loud cheer came from inside the bar, and he glanced over to see Tryptan had arrived, and Brin was wrestling the laughing fledgling toward the mass of celebrating Ascendants.

Kennex chuckled, "He's getting a little too good at sneaking out of the Nest."

"Brin pays off the guard," Lee replied, but her tone sounded distant.

Kennex turned back to her to see she was still staring into the bar, but her mind was clearly elsewhere. He pulled her hand from his face but kept it in his own. Kennex gave it a small squeeze and she snapped back into the moment.

"You okay?"

"Yeah. I just remembered." Lee shook her head. "Did I ever tell you about what I found on the recording device I placed on Tryptan on our trip to Upolent?"

"No. We got a little distracted," Kennex chuckled.

Lee grinned but it faltered, and she leaned back against the railing. "I found nothing." Kennex tilted his head and she continued. "As in, there wasn't anything."

"Maybe it was broken?"

"No, you can hear shuffling and background noises, but that's it. There's no conversation with a Stellotrian recorded on it, and it ends right before we caught up to him."

Kennex furrowed his brow. "Maybe the acid rain messed with it?"

"Maybe," Lee mumbled. She shrugged after a beat. "I mean, probably, but it was just weird."

"Let's just ask him about it." Kennex suggested with a step toward the glass door.

Whatever Lee planned to reply to him was interrupted by the shrill beeping of vambraces. All of them. His and Lee's went off simultaneously, and Kennex could see everyone inside the bar was also pausing to check their own. Lee was reading her message, but before Kennex could open his own, or even ask her, an alarm rang through the air followed by Malachi's voice summoning everyone to the Cathedral.

"How often does Malachi call a court wide meeting like this?" Kennex asked as a heavy stone settled in his gut.

Lee bit her lip before replying, "Never."

"This can't be good," Brin hummed.

Kennex looked over Lee's head, who sat pressed to his side, where Brin scanned the room. He agreed, but he wasn't sure why. Kennex only had a foreboding alarm ringing at the back of his head. They had all come straight from Rakerby's. Tryptan had to hold off and slip in with a pack of fledglings. Vira had already left the bar to seek out Lyris before the message had been sent out.

"Thank you for clarifying that for us, Brin," Lee snipped. She crossed her arms—fingers digging into her bare biceps. Kennex settled a hand on her shoulder in reassurance, but she only replied with a tense smile.

The room was filling up quickly and every eye seemed focused on the stage where a box sat. It didn't belong with the stone stage. The box was made of a light-colored wood that had been intricately carved and shaped. Portions were painted in a soft blue and green.

Kennex shook his head. "I'm sure everything is fine."

The words tasted like a lie on his lips, and he almost felt bad for offering out a reassurance he didn't believe.

"Oh, there's Vira."

He looked down the aisle they sat in to find Vira approaching. Her eyes were focused on the back of the room, and when Kennex followed her gaze, he spotted Lyris filing in. Under his attention, the adherent glanced his way, and he gave her a nod she returned.

"V, do you know what this is about?" Brin was the first to question.

"No," she sat down on Kennex's other side, "But that box is from Drucanna."

Kennex's head snapped back to the box. He squinted, focusing on the designs, and realized the box reminded him of Recluse's desk on Acheron.

"How do you know?" Lee asked.

"It's hand carved," Vira replied. "All those patterns on the side? They're war sigils." Kennex locked his jaw at her words. Vira's wary gaze flickered to him. "It's not a good sign."

Lee let out a quiet scoff. "Of course it isn't. Nothing good comes from Drucanna."

"That's not true." Brin chimed with a smile that didn't quite reach his eyes. "You like their frost wine well enough."

"Shut up, Brin."

The back and forth of the twins didn't have the same energy it usually did. Brin's jest was morose, and Lee's retort had no bite.

Finally, the room fell quiet as the stage opened, and Malachi rose up from below. Scattered applause began, but the man lifted his arms to silence it.

"Thank you for coming so swiftly, my flock," Malachi began. He stalked to the box and carefully placed his hands on the top. "It was vital I speak to you before the system claimed this story and rumors began." Anticipation hung in the air—heavy and foreboding. "There has been an incident."

"What the hells is this bastard talking about?" Brin murmured.

"It had been reported to me via message, but I didn't believe it—refused to believe it, I suppose." Malachi's voice cracked, but Kennex didn't believe the pain. The Stellotrian was a master of manipulation. *What is he trying to sell us?* Malachi cleared his throat. "There has been a death."

A quick whisper of confusion washed over the crowds, but Malachi did not leave the room in suspense. With a ragged cry of either rage or sorrow, he grasped the top edge of the box and threw it open.

Kennex didn't realize it was a coffin until the wooden lid clattered against the stage.

He didn't realize a body laid in it until the crowd exploded in cries of shock and pain.

Kennex didn't realize who it was until Lee screamed.

"Our esteemed Ascendant X'ael, our brother and friend, has been murdered!" Malachi roared. He threw his hands up and a digital image of

X'ael formed in the air. Not of him in his prime, but a close-up of his pasty and bloodied corpse. A gnarly wound ripped his throat open in swollen and bruised tissue. Lee wavered beside him, sobbing, and Kennex caught her by the elbow. Still, she collapsed to the ground with him clutching onto her.

The others were quicker than him. Brin knelt to his sister's side, holding onto her as she shook, and Vira was sprinting down the stone steps to the stage. Kennex was frozen. Sound around him seemed muffled as he studied X'ael's lifeless eyes. A sinking feeling dragged him under.

Kennex knew. He didn't know how he knew.

But he knew.

Vira was shouting at Malachi as she covered the coffin with the lid, but the Curator paid her no mind. He lifted his arm once more and this time when he spoke, Kennex could feel the starry gaze hidden under golden glass burning into him.

"He was murdered by this insurrectionist!"

Kennex pictured Ari's burning brown eyes before the image formed, but he still felt the air knocked from him when she appeared. Muffled sounds went mute and were replaced with a ringing—as if a bomb had imploded in his head.

Ari had white hair and black markings painting her left arm, that was new, but the anger drawn across her features was old. The image was a still taken from a video and heavily zoomed in based on the slight blur of the lines forming her.

Even so, she was unmistakable.

"Arienna Barlow!" Malachi yelled. "Arienna Barlow has taken X'ael from us! She leads a force that threatens to corrupt this system, to kill us, and destroy all the good Illyarium has always stood for!"

Kennex's knees went weak, and he fell back into his seat. Even with the row in front of him standing on their seats, he could see Ari's eyes above their heads. He could not escape her image, or Malachi's words.

"We will not stand for this! We will not allow Drucanna's legionaries to roll over us! We will find justice!"

Ari had been on a journey of her own, and Kennex feared the conclusions she had drawn. His desire to find her, to open her eyes to the entire situation at hand, and protect her from the threats on the horizon grew in his chest. It was painful how badly he needed to speak to her. Amid the determination came a haunting reminder in Vira's voice from a conversation that hadn't returned to him until this very second.

You can't save someone who doesn't want to be saved.

The ringing stopped.

The crowd was chanting.

The war had begun.

- EPILOGUE -

Kennex was thankful that on his first day in the court, they had taken him to the clinic in Adherent Village. The clinic the acolytes used was not one he would have reacted well to waking in—not that he had woken in Lyris' clinic all that well. Acolytes, as he learned, lived underground. Beneath the court were a series of complicated tunnels that created a maze-like city. Unlike Haven which was filled with light, warmth, and a sense of community, every area created for the acolytes kept an impersonal, detached environment. Tile floors, concrete walls, and an echoing silence.

The clinic he waited in was equally as plain. The antiseptic scent in the air was so strong it burned his nose, and every countertop, cabinet, cot, and piece of equipment was so blindingly white that it strained his eyes. Vira sent a message requesting he meet her here along with the instructions on how to find it in the first place. Kennex didn't understand why they couldn't meet anywhere else, and he only stayed out of respect for Vira and curiosity on where the hells she had been. Right after the announcement of X'ael's shocking death, she had left the court with only a vague explanation.

He heard her footsteps before he saw her. The clinic doors were locked in an open position, and Vira stepped in with a sigh. Her hair was damp and pushed back rather than pulled up in a usual bun.

Kennex slid off his chair. "V."

"Hey, new light. Long time no see." Vira cracked an exhausted smile.

"Where have you been? You've been gone weeks."

"Right into it, huh?" Vira replied. Kennex pressed his lips together and she nodded. "How is Lee holding up?" Kennex didn't respond, and Vira seemed to understand the answer. Badly. Lee was not handling the loss of X'ael well. Technically nobody in the court was. Ascendants seemed stunned and shocked as they went about their days. Loss in any shape was not an easy concept to come to terms with, but the immortals were unsurprisingly bad at it. "Right. I guess I shouldn't be too surprised. Lyris?"

Kennex nodded once. "She's fine." That had been Vira's only message prior to leaving: Watch out for Lyris. With Lee out of commission and Tryptan buried in more intense training, this fell to his and Brin's shoulders. "Vira, what is going on?"

"I had to go pick up an old friend," Vira sighed.

She motioned with her head for him to follow and he furrowed his brow when she led him deeper into the medium sized clinic. The entire space, like the many halls he perused, were empty. Vira walked up to a large cabinet that sat against a back wall and pulled the doors open. Kennex's eyes widened at the lift hiding there, but he didn't question it as they stepped in.

As they traveled deeper down, he allowed himself one question.

"Is every part of the acolytes living space this fraking creepy?"

"Yup," Vira replied.

The lift doors slid open into another plain hallway. However, other than their echoing steps, Kennex heard voices. They were the first he had heard down in the halls, and Vira seemed to be leading him directly toward them.

"—and where is she?"

"Are you *that* delusional? Even if I knew, even if I told you, do you really think she'd want to see you again?"

Two male voices, and Kennex did note that the deeper of the two was vaguely familiar to him. The voice he knew, but couldn't accurately recall, tried to speak again, but the other interrupted him with a snarl.

"Why are we here!? I want to see Primm. If you fraking touched a hair on her head—"

"Do you really think I'd let anyone hurt her? Do you really think that little of me? That I would be capable of that?"

"After Sziklam?" A harsh laugh bellowed. "I don't know what you're capable of anymore."

Vira slipped through a doorframe and Kennex followed into a large circular room. It matched the clinic with equipment that looked medical in nature, but Kennex couldn't ignore the cages that lined one wall. One sight did distract him from it though.

Derrik Russell.

Kennex's step stuttered as the Ascendant's full presence hit him. Derrik's bright green eyes snapped to him and narrowed into a glare, but Kennex stared in shock at the deep, jagged scar that cut across his face diagonally. His hair was longer than it was in the mural back on Acheron and he had the stubble of a beard recently shaved.

Kennex lunged.

It was instinct. His fist slammed into Derrik's face sending the Ascendant sprawling back. Another harsh laugh from across the room, but Vira's hand grabbed him by the back of the neck and yanked him away.

"What the hells are you doing?" Vira barked at him.

"Fulfilling a promise I made," Kennex spat. He shrugged out of Vira's hold with a nod that he was content. The promise he made Ari hadn't been one he spoke aloud. Really, it was a promise he made himself. That if he ever saw Ascendant Derrik Russell, he'd punch the immortal on behalf of the secondhand pain his partner suffered at the foot of his murals. Kennex and Ari had been drunk when she admitted her deep, dark secret to him, but a promise was a promise in his mind—no matter how ridiculous.

"Hit him again."

Kennex finally turned to take in the other man. He was on his feet, standing tense, but his hands were chained behind his back and connected to the wall. Blue eyes burned into him, and a cruel smirk crossed the man's lips.

"It's the least you can do for betraying your partner, Kennex *fraking* Hall."

Kennex stiffened. "What did you just say—"

"Spare me," he snorted. "We all saw your debut—"

"Ellis, shut up," Vira snapped.

Derrik had risen back to his feet with a huff, but Kennex's attention remained on Ellis. Blue eyes, reddish-blond hair, and Kennex noted his features were familiar. He pointed to him. "Rames. You're a Rames."

"Get fraked, screwhead," Ellis spat at him.

Kennex glanced between the two Ascendants then back to Vira, "What is this?"

"Reparations."

Kennex resisted the urge to blow a sigh at Malachi's voice, but Ellis held no self-control. He bit out a curse and pulled on his restraints. Vira grabbed Kennex by the elbow and dragged him to the side of the room away from the forming scene.

Malachi settled in front of Ellis with a sigh. "Oh, my poor lost son."

Ellis lunged toward Malachi, straining against the chains that tore skin and released gold light. "Where the frak is my daughter!?"

"She is fine, Ellis Rames," Malachi responded calmly, and Ellis bristled further. Kennex glanced at Vira hoping for clarification, but she watched Malachi with a locked jaw and glare.

His eyes found Derrik next only to realize the Ascendant was already staring at him. "I would never hurt a child." Malachi's voice was aghast. "The insinuation that I would is insulting, but I do understand your distress. I will forgive your words this time and reiterate that she is safe. Primm Holt. She is very polite for her age. Her mother must have raised her well."

"*Malachi—*"

"I said do not worry," the Curator hummed. "She is in the court with her grandmother. Ascendant Heleen Rames was ecstatic to finally meet her granddaughter."

Kennex watched as anger melted into panic and desperation. Ellis fell to his knees and bowed his head. A flash of X'ael knelt in front of Malachi came to him, but this Ascendant didn't cower or shake—he slumped as if the entire system had fallen on his shoulders.

"Please. *Please.*" Ellis' voice was strained, and it cracked as he begged.

"She's a kid. She has nothing to do with any of this. Just—Just let her go."

Derrik cleared his throat. "Malachi, I can take Primm to—"

"She stays," Malachi interrupted. "Ellis betrayed Aether, betrayed the light within him, perhaps his daughter will make a better Ascendant one day."

Ellis' head snapped up and Kennex felt agony as a witness. The father's eyes filled with hatred, he could almost hear the man's teeth grinding from across the room, but he stayed on his knees and hissed out his pleas one more time. "Malachi, please. Do what you want to me. I'll take it—I'll take whatever punishment you want but leave her out of this. It's me you're mad at. It's me you hate."

"Hate?" Malachi tsked. "Ellis, I do not feel hate. I'm not even angry. I am just *so* disappointed." He cupped the side of the Ascendant's face and used his other hand to rake his fingers through his hair. "I expected so much from you. Perhaps that was my mistake."

Kennex took a half step forward, but Vira was quick to lock him in place. She shook her head minutely.

"But mistakes can be corrected..." Malachi held Ellis' face tenderly between both hands. "And gifts given can be taken away."

- ABOUT THE AUTHOR -

J.J. Kang was born in the colorful, lawless swampland that is Florida, and she identifies as a disaster. She graduated from the University of Mary Hardin Baylor with a B.S. in Cellular Biology and a minor in Psychology. However, her heart has always belonged to the written word so she has traded in her lab coat to pursue her dream of being a published novelist.

Other than reading and writing, J.J. enjoys kickboxing, crochet, and binging TV shows on a streaming device when she absolutely should be working instead. Typically she can be found in her natural habitat of a local coffee shop downing her sixth cup of coffee as caffeine via IV is currently frowned upon.

Find me at www.jayjaykang.com

www.ingramcontent.com/pod-product-compliance
Lightning Source LLC
Chambersburg PA
CBHW070342010826
48976CB00017B/1119